AUTUMN AT THE STABLES ON MUDDYPUDDLE LANE

Heart-warming, uplifting romance

Etti Summers

CHAPTER ONE

Timothy crossed the road, stepped onto the pavement and took a deep breath. He felt so nervous that his stomach churned. Interviews weren't his strong point (he tended to get a bit tongue-tied and flustered) and he was dreading this one, more than any other. Possibly because he wanted the job so badly.

The email inviting him for the interview had instructed him to go to the staff entrance and press the buzzer, but when he located it around the side of the building, he paused for a moment, vainly trying to compose himself.

It was no use – he was more nervous than a turkey at Christmas. Deciding to simply get it over with, he held his thumb on the buzzer and tried not to hold his breath.

The door was answered by a lady in her fifties who smiled warmly at him.

'You must be Timothy. I'm Celia, one of the reception staff. Come through, they're waiting for you.'

Timothy gulped and followed her, yanking at his tie as though it were a hangman's noose around his neck, which if he was truthful, was exactly what it felt like.

'If you'd like to wait in here, Tina and Brandon will be with you shortly,' Celia said, showing him into a spacious office.

Timothy thanked her and headed for a seat, but changed his mind at the last moment. It wouldn't look good if he'd made himself at home; not only that, he also didn't want to be at a disadvantage by having to leap to his feet when they came in.

Thankfully, his wait was a short one. In less than a minute the door opened and the two partners (husband and wife team, he assumed from their joint surname) greeted him.

'I'm Tina...'

'And I'm Brandon.'

He shook hands with them both, expecting them to sit down behind the desk, but was surprised when Tina handed him a white coat.

'We thought we'd leave the formal bit until later. I know we're looking for a large animal vet, namely equine, but how do you feel about having a crack at what's in the waiting room?'

'Er, fine, yes, okay, I'd love to,' he stammered, hastily removing his suit jacket and shoving his arms through the sleeves of the overall.

'We've got a full waiting room by the looks of it,' Brandon said, and Timothy bit his lip.

Being a vet meant being put under pressure on a daily basis, but not this kind of pressure. He felt as though he was sitting his exams all over again. However, as soon as he stuck his head into the waiting room and saw the dogs, cats and other assorted creatures in pet carriers and cardboard boxes, he immediately snapped into professional mode.

'Who's first?' he asked his interviewers out of the corner of his mouth.

'Penny Shanklin. French Bulldog,' Tina replied. 'I'll be your nurse today if you need one,' she added.

Timothy called the dog's name and its owner brought the little black animal into the consulting room.

'What seems to be the problem today?' he asked, as the elderly gentleman scooped the dog up and popped her on the table.

'Are you the new vet?' the animal's owner asked.

'No, but I hope to be,' Timothy replied with a smile, holding his hand out for Penny to sniff. Her nose was cold and wet, and she snuffled his fingers. 'What can we do for you?'

'Booster,' Mr Shanklin said. 'And she needs her nails clipped.'

'I'm sure we can manage that,' Timothy said, picking up a small black paw and seeing that the claws were indeed rather on the long side.

In a little over ten minutes the dog had received her booster and had been given a manicure; she had also been weighed, and Timothy had checked her eyes, ears, and teeth, and had listened to her heart and lungs.

Penny was now hoovering up her reward of several dog treats for being such a good girl, and as soon as she'd left the consulting room Timothy was on to the next patient – a cat, this time, who had an unexplained cough – and then the next.

Five dogs, three cats, one rabbit, one hamster, a gecko, and an extremely large and hairy tarantula later, and the waiting room was finally empty.

'Fancy castrating a llama?' Brandon asked, just as Timothy assumed the hands-on part of the interview was done.

He considered his new suit trousers, new white shirt and polished loafers, and his heart sank. 'Great!' he said enthusiastically. 'What's the background?'

'Just kidding,' Brandon said. 'We've seen enough. Let's have a cup of tea first, then a quick chat. Do you like Penguins?'

'Only if someone holds their beaks while I examine them,' Timothy replied seriously, as he was invited to take a seat in the office. Although he liked all animals, birds weren't his favourite. He preferred bigger and more solid creatures, such as horses.

'Oh, ha, ha,' Brandon chuckled, and it was only when Celia brought in a tray of drinks and a packet of Penguins that Timothy realised the vet had been referring to the chocolate biscuits and not the birds. Thankfully, Brandon thought he'd cracked a joke, and Timothy wasn't about to set him straight. He took a sip of tea, feeling nervous once more.

'I see you're currently a locum,' Tina said, getting down to business. 'Is that why

you applied to Picklewick Veterinary
Practice?'

'Yes, I've been covering a maternity
leave,' he explained.

'I take it you're willing to relocate. Would
that be a problem?'

'Not at all. My brother lives in Picklewick,
so I'll move in with him.' Not that he'd
asked Harry yet, or had even told him he
was applying for a job here.

'Would that be Harry Milton, by any
chance?' Brandon asked. 'We did wonder
when we saw the surname.'

'It would.'

'He's a good bloke.' Brandon nodded his
approval.

Timothy agreed. His brother was one of
the best; although how he'd react if
Timothy actually landed this job was

anyone's guess. The main reason for Harry moving out of the family home in Cheltenham and buying the farrier business in Picklewick had been to give Timothy his independence. Yet here Timothy was, planning on getting a job in the same village as his brother and expecting to move in with him.

A solid half-hour grilling later, and the interview was finally over. Timothy hoped he'd done enough to impress the partners, but all he could do now was wait.

Feeling slightly sick – he'd been too nervous to eat breakfast this morning – he left his car in the practice's car park and decided to grab a sandwich before he headed home. He supposed he should also drop in and see Harry before he left. He didn't want his brother to find out about his job application second hand. From what Harry had told him, the village wasn't very big and word might soon get around.

Picklewick had a main street with some quaint little shops such as a florist, a baker, a butcher, and a convenience store. There was a small church, a community centre, a care home, and a pub called the Black Horse. Timothy hoped it was a good sign, because horses were his specialty.

Deciding against paying the pub a visit this early in the day – after the morning he'd had he might be tempted to sink a pint or two and, as he had to drive home, he thought he'd better not – he came to a halt outside a cafe and peered inside. It looked nice enough so he pushed the door open and went in, feeling thankful his interview ordeal was over and praying Tina and Brandon wouldn't take too long to get back to him.

Charity Jones checked the time before deciding she could pop into Blake's cafe for a take-out sandwich and a coffee without being late for her shift. Falling asleep earlier hadn't been part of her plan for today, but she'd been up since the crack of dawn mucking out stables, so when she'd squished down on the sofa intending to read for half an hour she had ended up having a two-hour nap. She'd woken up groggy and disorientated, and had forgotten to make a sandwich for work.

The wonderful smell of fresh coffee hit her as soon as she stepped inside, and she fished her reusable cup out of her bag. A double shot of caffeine would hopefully wake her up enough to get through the following eight hours.

There was a bit of a queue, so she stood patiently in line and studied the selection of sandwiches and baguettes in the chiller. Should she go for tuna and mayo, or spicy chicken, she wondered.

Automatically, she texted her sister to see what she would plump for.

Faith's response was immediate. **Ham**

Had ham yesterday.

Tuna. Everything okay this morning?

Charity thought back; this morning seemed such a long time ago. She shuffled forward a place as someone was served, and almost bumped into the guy in front. He turned to look at her and she mouthed 'Sorry' at him.

He smiled, a dimple appearing in each cheek, and she couldn't take her eyes off them. She hadn't seen him before, and wondered who he could be. Picklewick was a small village, where everyone knew everyone else, more or less. But it had its fair share of visitors to the area, so he was probably only passing through.

He was seriously good looking, about her age, with sandy blonde hair, and twinkly blue eyes. She looked away quickly when she realised she was staring at him, and glanced back down at her phone to reply to her sister.

Yeah, fine, Midnight was a pain

In what way?

He was being unruly, Charity messaged. **You need to ride him more**

Haven't got the time. I'll take him for a quick ride when I go to the stables later.

Charity let out a small sigh. It wasn't just time that was Faith's problem; it was a steadily declining interest. The sisters had ridden since they were small, and for the past ten years or so they'd been lucky enough to have their own horses. They kept them at the stables on Muddypuddle Lane in exchange for helping out with things like tacking up, taking classes, accompanying people on hacks, and doing many of the other things necessary to keep a riding school running smoothly. Petra, the stable's owner, was more than happy with the arrangement, as were Charity and Faith, but lately Faith was more interested in her boyfriend than her horse, Midnight.

A worm of worry worked itself into Charity's heart. She could sense change in the air, but she had no idea what she could do about it. It was only natural that Faith, the more outgoing of the sisters and the one who'd had loads of boyfriends and who relished going out and socialising, would one day meet the man of her dreams. Which subsequently meant she had less time for her horse, and presently she had even less inclination. Charity was relieved to know Faith was going to the stables later, because unfortunately she'd be at work, so she wouldn't be able to.

With another sigh she dropped her phone into her bag, then went to fish it out again when the ringtone sounded, before belatedly realising it wasn't **her** phone that was ringing. It belonged to the guy in front. That they both had the theme tune to **Black Beauty** as their ring tone made her smile.

He was next in the queue, and as they shuffled forward once more Charity began tapping her foot, wondering why this was taking so long. She needed to get going if she wasn't going to be late for work.

'*What?*' the guy in front cried, his phone to his ear, and Charity shot him a look. He was rather on the loud side, and for a second she wondered if he was one of those people who wanted the whole world to hear his conversation, before she realised he was genuinely shocked as his face broke into the widest smile she'd ever seen and his eyes lit up.

'Really? That's wonderful. Yes, yes of course. I've left my car in your car park, so I can be there in about ten minutes, if that's all right? Brilliant, just brilliant!

Thank you ever so much. You won't regret it.'

He stared at his phone for a second, his face shining. Then he turned around and made to leave, clearly not wanting to wait any longer in the queue. Charity was pleased he was going because it meant she was one step closer to getting her tuna baguette and coffee.

Suddenly she felt the guy grab her arms and swing her around, then he planted a smacker of a kiss on her cheek as he declared, 'I've got it, I've got the job! Woohoo!' He did a little dance, swinging her round again, and she couldn't help but smile at him even though she should have been appalled that a strange man would do such a thing.

'Congratulations,' she said.

'I can't believe it, I honestly can't believe it.' Then he must have realised he had hold of her, because he suddenly let her go and his face was a picture of contrition. But underneath she could tell he was still sparkling with excitement.

'Sorry,' he said. 'I didn't mean to...' The grin broke out again.

'It's fine,' she said, laughing at his obvious elation.

'I must dash, I've got to sign something or do something, or...I don't know.' He shrugged, his happiness so palpable that Charity couldn't help be pleased for him.

'Just out of curiosity,' she said, 'what job did you get?'

'I'm the new vet in Picklewick.'

Charity cocked her head to the side and studied him. That was interesting – she used Picklewick vets for her own horse, as did Petra. 'No doubt I'll see you around,' she said.

'I hope so.' He made a squeaking noise and hopped up and down on the spot. 'I can't believe I've got the job,' he cried again. 'I'm the practice's new equine vet. Did you hear that? **Me!** I'm going to be the equine vet for Picklewick Veterinary Centre. I can't believe it. Wow!'

Wow indeed, thought Charity. She couldn't believe it, either. Not only was this guy attractive and friendly, he also seemed to share her love of horses.

Abruptly Charity wasn't sure whether she actually did need a coffee to perk her up, because the perking had already been done.

CHAPTER TWO

Timothy dashed out of the cafe without waiting to be served, because he didn't want to waste one single second before returning to the practice. He couldn't believe they'd made the decision so quickly. It was barely an hour since he'd shaken their hands and slung his jacket in the car as he'd loosened his tie and removed it, relieved to feel a little more casual. Formal attire wasn't his thing. He was far happier in jeans and a tee shirt, and he hoped his discomfort in having to wear a suit hadn't shown.

He hadn't recognised the number when it came up on his phone, and he had been in total shock when he'd heard Tina's voice on the other end. His initial thought was that he'd forgotten something, but when she'd said he'd got the job, he had been so excited he'd grabbed the girl standing behind him in the queue and he'd kissed her.

It was inexcusable and he shouldn't have done it, but he'd been so damned happy and he'd wanted to share it with someone. Thankfully, she didn't seem to have been too upset, so hopefully he hadn't alienated her. She might well live in the village, or nearby, and the last thing he wanted to do was to start off on the wrong foot.

Obviously, she'd been taken aback at first, but then she'd smiled at him and for a few moments all thought of his new job was eclipsed by the most beautiful smile he'd ever seen.

However, he'd better concentrate now, because he had paperwork to complete and things to sort out – namely, his future.

It was another hour before he'd signed everything that needed to be signed and the various details had been hashed out, and he was free to go. Timothy now had a bullet to bite, and he suspected it would be a hard one; so it was with some considerable apprehension that he phoned his brother to give him the news. At least it was a fait accompli and not just a "by the way I've applied for a job in Picklewick and I thought I'd better tell you before someone else did" conversation which was what he'd originally been preparing for.

'Hi bro,' he began airily when Harry answered.

'Hello, Timothy, to what do we owe the pleasure—? Hang on a sec, Petra wants me.' Harry's voice became muffled and Timothy guessed he'd put a hand over the phone.

He could hear Harry replying to Petra, and while he waited he formulated what he was going to say to try to soften the blow.

It was hardly a blow, though. More of a shock. Hopefully a welcome one. Timothy wasn't proposing to invade Harry's space, just rent a bit of it for a while until he found somewhere to live. Although, it did seem rather daft to rent somewhere when there was a perfectly good room in his brother's cottage going spare.

'Sorry about that,' Harry said, coming back on the line.

'Are you at the stables?'

'Yes, why?'

'Just wondered.' Maybe it would be better to speak to Harry in person, with Petra there to diffuse the situation.

'Did you ring for a chat?' Harry asked. 'Because if so, can I call you back? Petra is having a problem with one of the horses.'

'Okay, no worries. I'll speak to you later,' Timothy said, and with that he got in his car and drove out of the village towards Muddypuddle Lane.

He'd visited the stables once before, back in the summer, curious to meet the woman who'd stolen his brother's heart. Before Picklewick, Timothy had begun to suspect Harry was a confirmed bachelor as he recalled Harry having had very few girlfriends, and it made him feel guilty to think Harry had sacrificed so much for him over the years, including his own chance of becoming a vet.

Harry had been in his second year of vet school when their parents had been killed. Timothy had just turned eleven. And for the past fourteen years, Harry had put his life on hold to parent Timothy. He'd given up his dreams and his youth. He'd tried to be both mother and father to a boy who'd had his world turned upside down and inside out, when he was barely more than a teenager himself. He'd fought to give Timothy as normal a life as possible, whilst putting his own on the backburner and struggling to keep a roof over their heads.

Now though, Harry had a thriving business after training to be a farrier, and had fallen in love with the prickly Petra, who wasn't half as cactus-like as she'd first appeared. It had been a love of horses which had drawn them together – that and Harry no longer having his little brother to hold him back.

Harry had told Timothy he'd moved out of the family home in order to give Timothy space and room to grow. He didn't need his older brother breathing down his neck, Harry had said. So as soon as Timothy had graduated and landed his first job, Harry had bought an established business shoeing horses and had moved to

Picklewick, leaving Timothy to spread his wings.

Timothy, however, had done enough wing-spreading whilst he'd been in university. And he might still be young (although twenty-four, nearly twenty-five, wasn't **that** young) but he felt it was now time to settle down. A new job and a new place to live would enable him to do that. Their home in Cheltenham, the one left to them by their parents and which he and Harry owned jointly, held too many memories. Within its walls he still felt like a little boy, lost and grieving.

He had already been looking for another job because the one he currently had was only a locum position, and he had been open to the possibility of relocating to anywhere in the UK, when he'd seen the advert for an equine vet in the same village his brother lived in.

He told himself it was fate, and ignored the very real worry that Harry had

escaped Timothy as soon as his
conscience would allow.

As Timothy drove the short distance from
the village to the stables on Muddypuddle
Lane, he pushed the worry to the back of
his mind and thought about handing in
his notice, putting the house in the hands
of a letting agent, and a hundred and one
other things, instead.

He pulled into the car park and got out,
scanning the empty yard as he did so,
and wondered where Harry could be.

Amos, Petra's uncle and the chap who
owned the stables, would probably be in
the house, so that was where Timothy
headed.

'Amos? Petra? It's Timothy,' he called as
he walked across the yard, adding,
'Harry's brother,' in case anyone had
forgotten.

'I know who you are, sonny,' Amos said, coming out of the tack room and wiping his hands on an old rag. He looked guilty and Timothy wondered what he'd been up to.

'They're down the bottom field,' Amos said. He glanced behind him nervously, then looked back at Timothy. 'Don't mention I was in there when you see Petra,' he said. 'She'll only tell me off, and what she don't know can't hurt her.'

'Why, what were you doing?'

'Best you don't know either, so you can't blab.'

Timothy tried not to smile. He should say something to Petra really, but he didn't want to cause any more waves than he was about to, and the elderly gent looked healthy enough. Harry had told him Amos suffered from angina and that Petra refused to let him do anything physical around the stables, so they employed a bloke called Nathan for the heavy work. Amos was relegated to doing the paperwork and the cooking, with the most energetic thing being to fork up the carrots in the veggie patch when they were ready for eating.

'I won't say anything,' he promised, earning himself a nod from Amos in return.

'It's lucky you showed up,' he said, and Timothy followed the direction of his gaze to see Harry and Petra walking up the field hand in hand. 'She'd have caught me, otherwise. Tell them I'm brewing a pot of tea if they're interested.'

Timothy strolled over to the fence at the edge of the stable block, rested his arms on it and stared out over the rolling countryside. The fields had lost their summer lushness and were turning pale gold, the colour triggered by the encroaching chill of the autumn air and the shortening of the days.

It was a beautiful spot: although it was just two miles from the village it felt as though the stables were in the middle of nowhere. The only habitation he could see were a few farms in the distance. The air was clean and fresh (if he ignored the aroma of horses) and the only sounds were the lowing of cows in a distant field and Petra's dog uttering the occasional bark as she nosed about in the undergrowth.

Harry and Petra were deep in conversation and Timothy was reluctant to make his presence known just yet, so they were almost in the yard before they noticed him. When Harry saw who it was, he did a comical double-take.

'What are you doing here?' he asked, releasing Petra's hand and pulling Timothy in for a hug. Petra patted him on the shoulder as she walked past, heading for the house.

'I've got some news,' Timothy said.

Harry stepped back. 'Oh?' He looked wary.

'I've got another job.'

'That's fantastic! Who with?'

Harry, Timothy realised, was assuming that Timothy would be working for one of the several veterinary practices in and around Cheltenham.

'Picklewick Veterinary Practice,' Timothy said.

'I'm sorry, I thought you said Picklewick.'

'I did.'

Harry froze. His expression was inscrutable and Timothy's already churning gut clenched. 'Why?' his brother asked eventually.

All the reasons Timothy had thought of when he debated what to say to Harry ran through his head and straight out again, until he was left with the only one that truly mattered. 'I miss you.'

'Aw, Tim…'

'I know, I know…I'm sorry.' He felt like crying. 'I'll tell them I've changed my mind. It's not too late, I haven't handed my notice in yet or—'

'Stop. Why would you do that?'

'Because you came here to get away from me and—'

'You silly sod!' Harry pulled him into another hug. 'I did **not** come here to get away from you,' he said indistinctly, his face buried in Timothy's hair.

'But I thought…'

'You thought wrong. I **told** you why.'

'I know what you said, but—'

'Do I ever say what I don't mean?' Harry leant back and grasped him by his upper arms.

'No?' Timothy felt as though he was a teenager again.

'Well, then. I moved to Picklewick so you didn't have me breathing down your neck.'

Timothy fell silent. It was true, that's what Harry had told him. 'You aren't mad at me?'

'Not at all. Now, tell me about this job of yours.' Harry slung an arm around his shoulder. 'And, more importantly, where are you going to live?'

'I thought I could move in with you for a while?'

'Now I really am mad at you. You do realise you'll be cramping my style?' his brother teased.

As Harry led him towards the house a weight lifted from Timothy's shoulders, and he buzzed with happiness. He simply knew he was going to love living in Picklewick.

'Is it cold outside?' Brian asked, when Charity wandered through the reception area heading towards the staff room to stow her bag and coat.

'It's fresh, but not too chilly. A typical autumn day,' she replied.

'I'd like to go for a walk.' The old man stared out of the window.

'Have you asked April?' April was the manager on duty today.

He shook his head.

'Would you like me to ask her for you?'

'If you wouldn't mind? I don't want to be any bother.' His expression was hopeful, with a hint of worry behind it.

Charity gave him a hug. 'It's not any bother. You must ask if you want something. We mightn't always be able to help, but if we don't know what you want we definitely **can't** help.'

'You're all so busy,' he pointed out.

'Busy trying to make everyone as happy as we can,' Charity said, smiling at him. 'And if going for a walk makes you happy...?'

'Can **you** take me?'

'I wish I could, but I have to be on reception. Tell you what, if it isn't possible for anyone to take you out today, I'll come in early tomorrow.'

'You're a good girl. Can we take my dog? He'd love a walk.'

Charity's heart went out to the old man. Brian's dog had been re-homed at the same time as Brian. The old man's family had suspected he'd been suffering from dementia for a while, and when he'd had a nasty fall and had to be hospitalised, their fears had been confirmed. Unable to look after himself any longer, he'd moved into the care home. Brian had been upset about his dog, but increasingly he forgot the little animal now had a new owner.

'I'll see what we can do,' she replied gently, not wanting to break his heart all over again by telling him he no longer had a dog. It was kinder this way, and by tomorrow he might well have remembered for himself.

'You're a good girl,' he repeated, and she felt tears prickle at the back of her eyes. Maybe she could ask Petra if she could borrow Queenie for a couple of hours? The spaniel loved people, and was soft-mouthed and gentle. Petra had brought her in before, and many of the residents enjoyed petting her. Thinking of Petra led Charity to think of the stables and the horses and ponies who lived there, and before she knew it she was thinking of Picklewick's newest vet.

Initially, she'd been shocked and rather perturbed at being accosted by a strange man, but he'd been so excited and so happy that she'd forgiven him immediately. No doubt she would see him around, and the knowledge had made her feel a little lightheaded.

Don't be silly, she told herself, as she settled in her chair behind the desk, her eyes running down the list of jobs she needed to do. He wouldn't be interested in her. A good-looking guy like him was bound to have a girlfriend. Charity had happened to be in the right place at the right time, that's all. If Brian had been standing behind him in the queue in the cafe, the guy would have done the same to him. Nevertheless, the attraction she'd felt refused to go away, and she wondered what his name was, where he lived and when she might see him again.

Cross with herself for wasting brain time on him, she tackled the first task on the list, and was soon on the phone confirming a delivery of supplies for the kitchen. Yet she still couldn't get him out of her head.

She tried telling herself he was far too exuberant for her taste, too confident and outgoing, more suited to Faith's personality than hers. Charity tended to go for shy, introverted men; not that she'd had many boyfriends, shy or otherwise, probably because both parties were too shy and introverted to ask the other person out. Besides, she didn't have a great deal of time for romance.

Storm, her horse, kept her busy, especially since Charity paid for the animal's board and lodge by helping out at the stables.

What with that and working at the residential home, it was tantamount to having two jobs.

'How's that horse of yours?' Olive asked, shuffling slowly through reception on her way to the lounge. Olive used to ride, Charity had discovered, and now relived her days in the saddle through Charity's stories of going on hacks or helping out with the riding lessons.

Olive stopped for a chat, and soon Charity had the old lady in stitches when she told her how Princess, the goat, had eaten one of Harry's favourite socks, and Petra had been on poop watch to make sure it came out of the other end of the goat and didn't cause the creature internal discomfort.

'You ought to have seen Harry's face when Petra asked him if he wanted the sock back,' Charity chortled.

Petra had mellowed considerably since Harry had arrived on the scene, and although she still generally preferred horses to people, she was now far more light-hearted and easy-going.

Charity hoped she could find a man like Harry one day – solid, dependable, grounded, kind, and rather attractive, too. Petra was a lucky woman.

A stab of envy caught Charity unawares, and she blinked at the unaccustomed emotion. For some reason, she found herself wishing she had someone special in her life, and she wondered what had brought that on. Not even loved-up Faith had made her feel she was missing something, yet here she was dwelling on love and romance.

What had gotten into her?

Unbidden, the face of Picklewick's newest vet swam into her head...

CHAPTER THREE

'Is this the last of it?' Harry asked, dumping the box none too gently on the floor of the spare bedroom.

'There's one more.' Timothy had been unloading the car and putting the assorted bags and boxes in the living room, and Harry had been helping by taking them upstairs. The pair of them were standing in what was now Timothy's bedroom and staring at the mess.

'You forgot something,' Harry said, shaking his head.

'What?' Timothy was pretty sure he'd packed everything he needed.

'The kitchen sink.'

'Ha, ha, very funny. You'd better stick to shoeing horses, because your stand-up comedy sucks.'

'I'll fetch whatever is left in the car,' his brother said. 'You make a start on this lot.'

Easier said than done, Timothy thought, putting his hands on his hips and blowing out his cheeks. Maybe he had been a bit excessive?

When **was** he going to have a kick about with a football? He hadn't played footie in a park since he was about eighteen, so what made him think he was going to do so now? And he was never going to listen to his old collection of CDs, was he? He didn't even like that kind of music anymore and neither did he have anything to play them on. He'd been so focused on getting the house cleared of anything personal, valuable or sentimental in order for it to be rented out, that he'd blindly packed anything he didn't intend to leave.

'Blimmin' heck, I reckon this one **does** contain the kitchen sink,' Harry said, letting a rather large box slip to the floor with a thud.

Timothy stared at it. 'That's Mum and Dad's stuff.'

'Ah.' Harry fell silent, and Timothy recalled the two of them going through their parents' things, trying to decide what to keep and what should be given to the charity shop.

Timothy had cried at the time, but Harry had remained stalwart. It was only later, long after Timothy had gone to bed that he'd heard his brother sobbing.

'Do you want to keep it in here?' Harry asked after a while. 'Or should I put it in the attic?'

'Attic,' Timothy said.

'Righto.' Harry clapped his hands together and set to work.

'I feel like we're the brothers in **All Creatures Great and Small,**' Timothy said sometime later, when Harry had taken yet another box up to the attic, tutting as he did so. 'I'm Tristan and you're Siegfried.'

'I hope you're **not** like Tristan,' Harry said. 'He was an irresponsible so and so. And don't you go playing around. Picklewick is a small place, and the female population doesn't need you trying to get into its knickers every five minutes.'

'I'm not like that!' Timothy protested.

'How many girlfriends have you had?' Harry countered.

'I can't help it if women find me irresistible,' Timothy said, then ducked when Harry threw a trainer at him.

'Seriously, I won't embarrass you,' he added, putting the trainer in the bottom of the wardrobe and wondering what had happened to its twin. 'I'm not a student any more.'

'I know. I can't believe you're all grown up.'

'I can't believe you're so old,' Timothy teased.

Ah, here it is, he thought, as he dodged another flying missile in the form of his trainer's mate.

'It's Tina and Brandon I feel sorry for,' Harry said. 'They don't know what they've let themselves in for.' And Harry chuckled as the trainer flew back across the bedroom.

'Stop being so childish,' Harry said.

'You started it.'

'No, I didn't.'

'Yes, you did,' Timothy argued.

Oh, this was going to be so much fun, Timothy thought. Away from Cheltenham and the family home which was now in the hands of a letting agent, his brother seemed lighter-hearted, more carefree. And he didn't think it was solely down to Harry relocating – if that's what being in love did for a fella, Timothy wouldn't mind finding the woman of his dreams, either.

An image of the girl in the cafe popped into his mind and he wondered whether he'd meet her again. He thought it was quite likely, especially if she had a pet.

Now that he'd officially moved to Picklewick, it might be a good idea to start getting to know the area and its residents. He had a couple of days before he had to report for work, so maybe he could pay a visit to Petra's stables. Riding was a great way of getting about, and he'd see far more from the back of a horse than he would if he drove, and he could cover more ground than if he walked. Besides, he loved riding and he hadn't done enough of it lately.

'Do you think Petra would take me on a hack?' he asked.

'I'm sure she would. Give her a ring.'

'Couldn't you ask her for me?'

Harry narrowed his eyes. 'How old are you – ten? Ask her yourself. She doesn't bite.'

'I don't like to impose.'

'You aren't. You're family as far as she's concerned.' Harry flattened a box, then looked at him.

'Will you two get married, do you think?' Timothy asked.

'Possibly. I'd like to think so.' Harry was thoughtful. 'I've been on my own for so long, that being in a relationship is taking a bit of getting used to. Both for me and for Petra.'

'I'm sorry.'

'For what?' Harry's expression was perplexed.

'For holding you back. I should have gone to live with Aunty Emma and Uncle Colin.'

'Don't be daft. You didn't hold me back. When Mum and Dad died, I wanted to look after you. I still do.'

'I don't need looking after,' Timothy objected, rolling his eyes, and once more the mood lightened.

He'd made the right decision in accepting the job and moving in with Harry, Timothy thought with a contented sigh. It was wonderful to see his brother so happy, and Timothy had a feeling he was going to be happy living here, too.

'Hi,' Timothy said warmly. He recognised the woman at once as the one from the cafe, and he felt a glow of pleasure. He'd only moved in a couple of days ago and he'd been hoping to bump into her. Surprised and pleased to discover she worked in the stables, he smiled broadly.

She returned his smile but there was no recognition behind it.

'I'm the new equine vet,' he said, hoping to prod her memory. 'Timothy Milton. Harry's brother,' he added in case she didn't make the connection.

'Hi, Timothy, nice to meet you. I'm Faith.'

'Actually, we, um...' He'd been about to remind her that they'd already met, but he decided not to bother. It hadn't been one of his finer moments, leaping on a total stranger. And he hadn't realised he was so forgettable either, and the knowledge knocked him down a peg or two; he was unused to such indifference from the opposite sex, although he did notice her look him up and down. He settled for, 'Nice to meet you, too.'

'If you wait here, I'll go fetch the horses,' she instructed, and left him loitering in the yard.

He watched her walk away, her hips swaying, her back straight, her hair stuffed underneath her riding cap to reveal the column of her soft white neck...Man, she was cute. Although, she seemed a little different to the woman he'd leapt on in the cafe, sharper somehow. He'd got the impression she was the typical sweet girl-next-door, but now he hastily revised his opinion. This woman was aloof, confident, spikier than he remembered. That would teach him to make assumptions about someone who he'd had only a fleeting contact with.

He could hear Petra's voice coming from the indoor arena and he guessed there must be a lesson going on, but of his brother and Amos there was no sign.

However, Nathan, the guy who was employed to do much of the heavy work, was driving a tractor up the lane, and he nodded at Timothy, who nodded back. The man was in his mid-to-late forties and as reticent as the vehicle he was driving, but Harry had told him he was a sound bloke and his actions spoke louder than words. Nathan might not say much, but he got the job done (whatever it might be) with the minimum of fuss.

'Petra tells me you've ridden before,' Faith said, coming around the corner leading two horses. One was a sizeable black gelding, the other a more delicate-looking thoroughbred mare. He assumed the gelding was for him.

'I've done a bit of riding, yeah,' he said, not wanting to blow his own trumpet. When his parents were alive, he used to compete most weekends.

'You won't need a leg up, then,' she said, handing him the mare's reins and going around the side of the gelding to lengthen the animal's stirrups.

'Let me do that,' he offered, wanting to make sure the length was right for his legs.

'You can do your own,' she told him, gathering the reins, sticking her foot in the stirrup and bouncing as she swung herself into the saddle. The gelding tossed his head and crabbed to the side.

Timothy looked at the mare, who gazed back at him impassively. She was an altogether calmer proposition.

'Are you sure you want to ride him?' Timothy asked Faith, as she shortened the reins even further to prevent the gelding from dropping his head. The horse pranced in annoyance at being thwarted.

'I think I should, considering he's my horse,' she replied with a smirk.

Timothy groaned inwardly – he was making assumptions again. Saying that though, the horse she was riding suited her.

'Walk on,' she told the horse, not waiting for him to mount up, and he found himself hopping on one leg as the mare began to move off before he'd managed to swing himself into the saddle.

Shaking his head at her, he pulled his horse to a stop, mounted, then followed the gelding. Soon they were on the open moorland above the stables with a chill westerly wind in his face, and he started to relax, contentment seeping into his heart as he felt himself gel with the mare and move with her gait.

There was only one small cloud on the blue sky of his horizon, and that was the rider in front of him. Clearly she wasn't into him at all – which was a pity, because for some reason she'd stuck in his mind and he'd been looking forward to getting to know her better.

Charity uttered a deep sigh as she gazed out of the window. Petra had phoned her earlier to ask how she was fixed for going on a hack later today, but she had been getting ready for work, so she'd suggested Petra asked Faith, as it was her twin's turn to be at the stables this afternoon.

She really wished she didn't have to go to work. Although she enjoyed her job, the day was a lovely crisp autumn one, and she would have loved nothing better than to have taken Storm out. She'd visited the stables this morning to muck out and clean some tack, but she hadn't had enough time to go for a ride.

Never mind, there was always tomorrow. Maybe she'd get up extra early, so she could get her chores done and saddle up her horse. She tried to ride her every day, but it wasn't always possible.

At least the latter half of the afternoon shift tended to be less busy than the mornings, and by the time seven o'clock arrived and she was on her break in the staff room, Charity had worked her way through her to-do list and was looking forward to a calm evening.

She had just made herself a hot drink and had settled down with her sandwiches when her mobile rang. It was her sister.

'How was the hack?' Charity asked before Faith had a chance to say anything.

'Oh, um, good. Harry's brother is a bit of a dish,' Faith said.

'When did you see **him**?' Charity had heard he'd moved in with his brother and the grapevine had also informed her he was due to start work at the vets shortly, but she had yet to bump into him.

'This afternoon. He was the guy I rode with.'

Charity's mood dimmed. She would have loved to have gone on a hack with Timothy. Work had got in the way, she thought grumpily, then she felt incredibly mean when she saw Mrs Routledge shuffling forlornly along the path leading from the outside seating area to the residents' entrance, and Charity made a note to sit with her for a while. The old lady had moved in only last week and she was feeling the loss of her home and her independence keenly.

'If I wasn't madly in love with Dominic, I'd fancy him myself,' Faith was saying. 'As well as being seriously good-looking, he's really friendly and he's smart.'

Everyone, especially men, responded to Faith in the same way, probably because of her outgoing personality. People tended to be more reserved around Charity, which was undoubtedly a reflection of her shyness. How could she expect a man to have a scintillating conversation with her, when she could barely look him in the eye?

Charity would bet her last penny that if Timothy was going to fancy anyone in Picklewick it would be Faith. Unluckily for him, Faith was smitten with Dominic so she wouldn't look at the new vet twice.

'Too friendly, I thought,' Faith was saying. 'I was a bit standoffish, though. I didn't want to give him any ideas.'

'What's he like as a rider?' Charity asked.

'Trust you! Here's me saying that a good-looking chap has rocked into town, and all you can think of is how well he rides.' Faith chuckled down the phone. 'He's pretty good, actually. Decent seat, and I'm not referring to his backside, although he did fill out his jodhpurs nicely.'

Heat stole into Charity's cheeks as she thought about Timothy's behind. She'd caught a glimpse of it as he'd dashed out of the cafe the day he'd found out he had the job, and even in a pair of suit trousers it had looked rather trim.

'He rode Storm and handled her like a dream,' Faith said, and Charity's blush deepened as she thought about him sitting astride her horse. Then she fanned herself with her hands and blamed it on the heat in the care home. It was usually warm, and Charity was often glad she was based in reception, as the doors to the main parking area were always opening and closing, letting in a constant stream of fresh air.

'Midnight was a nuisance, though,' Faith added. 'I should have swapped horses and ridden yours. Midnight could do with a firm hand, and this guy seems to know what he's doing.'

'I'll look forward to meeting him,' Charity said, muttering, '**Again**,' under her breath. For once, Charity hadn't shared everything with her sister. For some reason she'd not told Faith about him kissing her in the cafe. She tried to tell herself it was because she hadn't had the opportunity, but that was a lie; as was the excuse that it had slipped her mind – it hadn't.

She'd thought about him a lot as the weeks passed and the date for his arrival in Picklewick grew closer. She'd daydreamed and played what-if, envisioning their next meeting, and how delighted he would be to see her again.

In reality though, she guessed he would have totally forgotten her, and even when he was reminded he'd still be none-the-wiser. Besides, he'd met Faith now, and what man wouldn't prefer the more out-going sister.

Charity emerged from her reverie to discover there was an unaccustomed silence on the other end of the phone, and suddenly her senses were on high alert. Something was wrong – there was an atmosphere which hadn't been there a second ago.

'I need to tell you something. It's the reason I phoned.' Faith sounded sheepish and hesitant. Not like her usual confident self at all.

A horrible feeling welled up inside her, and Charity desperately didn't want to hear what Faith was about to say. She felt sick, her half-eaten sandwich resting heavily in her stomach. This wasn't going to be good – she felt it in her bones.

'Dominic has asked me to move in with him,' Faith said.

Was that all? Relief surged through her: trust her to get worked up over nothing. Charity wasn't surprised at the news. 'You practically live at his house already,' she said, 'so it makes sense.'

'He's got a new job.'

Something in her sister's voice sent a shiver down Charity's spine. Why should a new job matter?

'It's in Norwich,' Faith continued. She sounded upset, and the shiver turned into a tremor. Was Faith distressed because she didn't intend to move halfway across the country with Dominic, and therefore their relationship was over? Or – and this thought made Charity's blood run cold – was Faith anxious because she **did** intend leaving Picklewick and her family, and things would never be the same again? Charity began to well up and she chewed at her lip.

Faith said, 'I'm sorry to land this on you over the phone, but he only just rang me and told me about the job. I simply had to speak to you **now.**'

'What are you going to do?' Charity asked, sniffing, her eyes stinging with unshed tears. She understood why Faith hadn't wanted to wait to tell her face to face. If the shoe had been on the other foot, Charity would also have wanted to share the news with her twin immediately.

'I love him,' Faith said, and the simple sentence told Charity everything she needed to know.

'Then you have to go with him. I would.'

'Would you?'

'I would.' Charity nodded emphatically, even though her sister couldn't see her. She wasn't being strictly truthful, but Faith didn't need to hear her doubts and reservations; her twin needed to follow her heart. There **was** one thing Charity wanted to know, though. 'If you don't go, would Dominic leave Picklewick anyway?' she asked.

'No. He'll stay.'

'Is it a good job? One worth moving for?'

'Definitely. He's been dreaming about a job like this ever since he left university.'

'He must love you very much,' Charity observed.

'He does.'

'So the question you should ask yourself is, do you love him as much?'

'I do – I really do.'

'Then you must go. You'll easily get another job – it's not as though you're wedded to the one you've got,' Charity observed.

'I don't want to leave you,' Faith cried.

And Charity said the hardest thing to ever pass her lips. 'Faith, my darling, you already have.' She was thankful Faith couldn't see her face, because she was falling apart inside. 'I'm so pleased for you,' she said, gulping back tears and hoping her distress couldn't be heard over the phone.

'Thanks. Shit!' Faith's voice was strangled. 'I said I wasn't going to cry.' She let out a sob which immediately set Charity off, and she put the rest of her unwanted sandwich to the side and staggered over to the sink for some kitchen roll to stem the flow.

When the sobbing had reduced to sniffles and Charity could speak again, she said, 'Have you told Mum?'

'Not yet. I wanted to speak to you first, to see what you thought. There wasn't any point in upsetting her, if I decided not to go.'

Charity felt tearful all over again; to think if she hadn't been so supportive Faith might have decided to remain in Picklewick, where she wouldn't be happy without the man she loved.

'I'll talk to her and Dad this evening,' Faith promised. 'I know they'll be pleased for me.'

As am I, Charity thought. And she **was**. Faith deserved every ounce of happiness in the world. 'How long before you leave?'

'Two months, maybe? I think Dominic will be starting his new job in January.'

So soon? Charity felt lost, as though her anchor had been pulled up and she was drifting out to sea, alone and rudderless.

What was she going to do without her sister? She had always been one half of a pair, but now the other half was aligning herself to someone else and Charity didn't know how she was supposed to bear it.

'Smile lovey, it might never happen,' Brian said, as she emerged from the staff room, red-eyed and shaking some time later.

'Actually, Brian, I think it already has,' she told him, earning herself a confused glance as he hurried off to find someone more cheerful to talk to.

CHAPTER FOUR

Charity adored dressing up, and Halloween was as good a reason as any. She had bought her costume and that of her horse ages ago, and had been looking forward to it, but the news that Faith had dropped on her had driven all thoughts of the party out of her mind.

Faith wasn't as keen on fancy dress, and Charity wondered if it had something to do with their different personalities. Charity enjoyed hiding behind her costume and mask: Faith didn't appear to need to, so what her sister wore tended to be more sexy vamp than a bandaged mummy, which is what Charity had dressed up as last year for the Halloween party. It hadn't been her best look, she admitted, and the bandages had been far too hot and restricting.

This time she was going as a skeleton, with an all-in-one stretchy suit which made her look like she was nothing but bones in the dark (the white parts of the fabric were slightly luminous) and Faith had done her make-up for her, so her face now looked like a skull. She thought she was the epitome of Halloween. It also suited her bleak mood perfectly.

The party was being held at the stables; it was mainly for the younger ones, but she always dressed up for it and she knew many of the parents would be in costume too. She'd even painted white bones on her horse (somewhat inexpertly) so Storm, who was a very dark bay, looked like a skeleton horse if she squinted and the light was poor – which it would be in the arena later. The place had been kitted out with battery-operated lanterns in the shapes of pumpkins, skulls and other assorted Halloween-y things ready for the scary ghost stories at the end of the evening.

Charity, Faith and Petra had taken ages to decorate the arena, and that was after Petra and Nathan had done the hard work of humping bales of hay around and setting up the indoor games. Amos had provided a buffet in the viewing gallery, out of the reach of whiskery noses and equine curiosity. It was shaping up to be a great evening.

Storm was still in her loosebox, so Charity went to fetch her, and giggled when she saw the mare's long-suffering expression. The horse didn't look particularly pleased with being painted, and as Charity saddled her, she kept glancing around at her rump as though she couldn't believe what she was seeing.

'Come on, girlie,' Charity murmured, 'You'll enjoy yourself – you always do.

And Amos has baked some horsey treats for you.'

Storm's ears pricked up and not for the first time Charity had the impression the animal understood what she was saying.

Faith was already in the arena, supervising the arrivals, Midnight tethered to a post by her side and contentedly munching on some hay. The other ponies had been brought out and had been "dressed" for the occasion, and the space was filling up with excited children and their parents.

Before Petra allocated each child a mount, the first competition took place, which was the best costume, followed by the best parent and child costume, then the funniest outfit, plus several more, until each child had a small prize. Harry had been roped in to judge and he was resplendent as a wizard, complementing Petra's witchy outfit.

Faith, Charity noticed, had slipped away soon after, having done her duty by showing her face. Charity felt slightly resentful: it was yet another sign that Faith was gradually distancing herself from the stables. What worried Charity was the fear that Faith was distancing herself from her, too. They'd always sworn no man would ever come between them, but Faith was in love, and Charity, to her shame, felt left out. The fact that Faith was disappearing off to Norfolk next weekend for a couple of weeks in order to sort out accommodation and to attend an interview or two, didn't help Charity's glum mood.

Deliberately pushing her negative thoughts away, she plastered a smile on her face and determined to be as cheerful as possible this evening for the children's sakes. They didn't deserve to see her miserable face, and neither did Petra. After all, Charity admonished herself silently, it wasn't as though she wasn't pleased for her sister – she was thrilled to bits for her. It was her own fault she was feeling so down; she relied on Faith too much and Charity had been guilty of being content to live her life vicariously through her twin.

It was time Charity made more of an effort with socialising, and it was probably a good idea if she paid less attention to her horse and put more energy into finding a boyfriend of her own, then perhaps she wouldn't feel so left behind.

Petra was about to start the games, beginning with a spooky egg and spoon race where riders balanced a plastic eyeball on a spoon whilst steering their ponies around a line of poles, when Charity spotted a familiar face. Timothy, the new vet, had come dressed as the Grim Reaper. The cloak and the cowl suited him, and she noticed he had let his beard grow a little. To Charity, he looked as though he belonged in Middle Earth, and to her consternation she came over all giddy.

Thanking her lucky stars he was too busy watching the first game to notice her and her furious blushing at how attractive she found him, Charity checked that the stables' version of ducking for apples was ready to go. The apples hung at face height (if you were astride a horse, that is) and it took skill for the children to grab the apple with their mouths, whilst keeping the horse still and not falling off. Last year, Parsnip, a creamy coloured cob, had managed to sink his teeth into the apple before his rider had a chance, leading to much hilarity.

Charity was hoarse from shouting encouragement by the time the final competition was over, and her sides ached from laughing. She loved these events, seeing the shining faces of the children and the pride of their parents, but this evening there was an extra zing to the atmosphere, a zing no one but her could feel, and that was because of Timothy.

He'd finally noticed her underneath all the paint, and had sent her a smile which she'd returned, glad that the black and white make-up hid her blushes.

She didn't think it could hide the confusion she felt about him though, and she hastily looked away, hoping he couldn't tell how much she was attracted to him. But she couldn't help glancing back at him again, only to find he was still watching her, and it made her quite light-headed – until she realised he probably thought she was her sister. Her outgoing, confident, sparkling sister.

Her spirits suitably dampened, Charity grabbed hold of the reins of the nearest pony and took him to his stable to be bedded down for the night.

My word, that was fun, Timothy thought when the games drew to a close with a hunt-the-spider event which was the same as an Easter egg hunt but without the chocolate goodies and with a great deal more squealing.

Petra's ponies were patient creatures, well used to the antics of the children who rode them, and hardly flicked an ear when their riders shrieked at the sight of a plastic spider.

'I can't touch it, Daddy,' cried one little girl, and Timothy hurried over to help her.

'I'm Timothy and I'm a vet, so I'm used to picking up spiders,' he told her, smiling at the child's father. 'What's your name?'

'My name is May, and this is Tango. He's older than me but he doesn't like spiders, either.'

Timothy reached up to remove the plastic spider from the top of a pole and popped it into the basket Petra had given each child. Tango, despite the little girl's conviction that the pony didn't like spiders, didn't bat an eyelid.

'How many have you got?' he asked her, and she counted.

'Seven.'

'That means seven sweets. Well done!' Petra, rather than hide sweets in the arena where any forgotten ones might be discovered by Queenie, her spaniel, or by one of the ponies, had hidden loads of fake spiders around the place, which would be exchanged for sweets to eat after the buffet.

Thinking of the buffet made Timothy's stomach growl. He'd come straight from work and was starving. He'd only had time to change into his Death costume, complete with scythe which he was unduly pleased with because he thought it gave him an edgy look, before he'd hightailed it to the stables.

As soon as he'd entered the arena (which was wonderfully decorated) he had been accosted by a cacophony of children's voices, the smell of hay and horses, and by the sight of Faith.

He'd spotted her within the first few seconds, and he thought how sexy she looked dressed in a figure-hugging skeleton costume. She'd painted her face to look like a skull and her long dark hair was piled loosely on the top of her head. She'd even painted a horsey skeleton on Storm, although why she was riding the mare and not Midnight flummoxed him for a moment until he realised the gelding might be too flighty.

He'd smiled at her and she had smiled back, then she'd looked away, before glancing back at him again, which had made him wonder if she was flirting with him. He thought she might be, but he wasn't convinced; if she was, he didn't appreciate the hot and cold approach. He decided to give her the benefit of the doubt, though – maybe she had her reasons for being so distant the other day.

Finally, the games were over and it was time to eat, and he was about to head to the viewing gallery when he realised Harry, Nathan and Petra were leading the ponies out of the arena, and Faith had already left. Guessing she was seeing to Storm, he helped May dismount from Tango, lifted the reins over the animal's head and led the pony outside.

'Where does this one go?' he asked, meeting Faith as she was walking back to the arena. Hopefully she'd bring another pony out and they could unsaddle them together, but when he glanced over his shoulder he realised there were no more mounts left inside.

'Fourth stall from the end,' she said, and he noticed she gave him only a swift look before averting her eyes.

'Thanks,' he said, convinced she was definitely flirting when he took a step in the direction of the row of stalls, and he saw her peep at him again.

By the time he'd unsaddled Tango, brushed him down, and had made sure the pony had a hay net to munch on, the buffet was in full swing.

Timothy grabbed a plate and piled it with food, and as he did so the main lights overhead went out, leaving only the lamps for illumination. Most people were sitting on a pile of bales in one corner which had been arranged in a semi-circle around a single point, and it was to the figure sitting on her own that his attention gravitated.

Faith had an open book in her lap, and she began to read.

Drawn to her like one of the moths fluttering around the lanterns, Timothy perched on the edge of a bale, his food forgotten as he listened to her weaving tales of ghouls and ghosties and things that went bump in the night.

Mesmerised, he gazed at her without embarrassment, and as he did so he realised he was more attracted to her than he'd ever been to any other woman he'd met.

He just hoped she was attracted to him, too.

'The End,' Charity whispered and closed the book with a snap that made her avid listeners jump, then giggle. She waited a moment for the children and their parents to gather themselves, then she nodded to Petra to switch on the overhead lights.

Blinking owlishly at the abrupt brightness, she stretched and got to her feet. It might be time for most people to leave, but she'd stay to help Petra tidy up. Even though the horses were safely tucked up for the night, there was still a great deal to do, from putting away all the poles and returning the bales to the barn, to clearing away the paper plates, and raking the arena so it was fit for lessons tomorrow.

Technically, she wasn't expected to do any of it, but she wanted to. She had nothing to rush home for and she'd only be scrunched on the sofa with a book if she left now. Besides, Timothy was still there, and at this very moment he was hoisting a pole and Petra was showing him where it lived.

Reaching for a black bag to put the rubbish in, Charity began collecting up plates and cups, and as she was doing so she was acutely conscious of Timothy –

where he was, what he was doing, how gorgeous he looked dressed as the Grim Reaper, how the short beard suited him...

All through her reading, she'd been acutely conscious of his eyes on her, making her glow from the inside out, making her heart race and her fingers tingle. He'd kept his attention on her the whole time, and she'd had to fight not to lose her place in the story. The goosebumps which had sprung up on her arms didn't have anything to do with the scary tale, and had everything to do with the way he was looking at her, until she was reluctant to lift her head from the book as she read, in case he realised the effect he was having on her.

'It was a good evening,' he said, materialising at her elbow and making her jump. Clearly she'd not been as in tune with his whereabouts as she'd thought she was, letting him creep up on her like that.

'It was,' she agreed, keeping her gaze downwards as she searched for more rubbish.

'Hold the bag open,' he instructed, and when she did as he asked and he popped the core of an apple into it, his hand brushed hers, sending desire surging through her veins.

It was so unexpected and so unlike her, that she gasped, and he snatched his hand away.

'Sorry,' he muttered.

'It's okay, you made me jump, that's all.' As explanations went, it was a poor excuse for one and he shot her a curious glance.

'How long have you worked here?' he asked, falling into step next to her as she trailed around the arena.

'I don't actually work here,' she said. 'I stable my horse in exchange for mucking out, teaching the odd lesson, and so on. I work in the care home in Picklewick as a receptionist.'

'I bet it's rewarding,' he said.

'Sometimes. It's hard when you lose a resident though.'

'I hate losing patients too.'

'How are you settling in?'

'Great, thanks. The practice is fab, and I love my work. Harry's not a bad landlord either, when he remembers not to leave his dirty socks on the bathroom floor.'

'Oi! I heard that, and those socks, my friend, were yours,' Harry chuckled.

'Were they?' Timothy scratched his chin. 'I could have sworn they were yours.'

Harry bumped Timothy's elbow as he walked past. 'I'm going to check on the horses with Petra and then I'm going to turn in for the night. Make sure you lock up when you get home.'

'I take it you're spending the night here?' Timothy asked.

'Yep. See you tomorrow, little brother. Night.'

'Night,' Timothy called, as Charity gave Harry a small wave. 'Are you off home, too? Can I give you a lift?'

'I've got my car, but thanks anyway,' she told him. 'I have a few more things to do here, so you might as well get going. Thanks for your help.' She nodded at the almost full rubbish bag in her hand.

'If you're sure...?' He paused. 'I really enjoyed the hack the other day,' he said.

'Good.' Her tone was non-committal, but her heart dropped to the soles of her riding boots. Great – he was sounding her out about Faith. That was why he was hanging around.

'Do you think we could go out again?'

'You'll have to ask Petra,' Charity said.

'I'll do that,' he said. 'No doubt I'll see you around?'

'No doubt,' she replied stonily, disappointment oozing from every pore as she watched him leave.

And when Petra locked the arena doors a short while later and said goodnight to her, Charity's fears were confirmed when Petra said, 'Timothy wants to go on another hack – I take it he's okay to ride Storm again?'

Numbly Charity nodded. It made no difference that Faith was in a relationship

and that she wouldn't look twice at him –
the fact that he was interested in her
sister and not her, was the issue. Which
was a pity, because she really fancied
him and for a while she'd got the
impression the fancying was mutual.

Down in the dumps and feeling rather
sorry for herself, Charity made her way
home, thinking that the closest she was
ever going to get to Timothy was sharing
her horse with him.

How sad was that?

CHAPTER FIVE

Because the Black Horse was the only pub in Picklewick, it was usually busy, especially on Friday nights and at the weekend. On this particular Friday the twins were enjoying a drink together because Faith was about to depart for Norwich tomorrow for two weeks and this might be their last chance to catch up for a while.

They might both still live at home, but lately it had been a technicality on Faith's part as Dominic was renting a place of his own, so Faith spent most of her time there.

Of course, the sisters phoned and messaged each other constantly, but it wasn't the same as one of them popping into the other's bedroom before they went to bed, or chatting over a bowl of cereal at breakfast, or exchanging gossip as they helped their mum make dinner.

In fact, Charity was having difficulty remembering the last time they'd done anything like that, because Faith was hardly ever at home these days.

They used to be so close they knew what the other was thinking, more or less living in each other's pockets, but gradually as their jobs led them in different directions, and then as Faith began to fall in love with Dominic, they saw less of each other. And it didn't help that Charity worked shifts, and they took it in turns going to the stables, so their paths crossed less and less.

Sometimes Charity thought that if it wasn't for the fact they were identical twins and she saw Faith's face staring back at her whenever she glanced in the mirror, she would have forgotten what her sister looked like.

Okay, maybe she was exaggerating, but Charity couldn't help feeling sad that Faith was moving on with her life and leaving Charity behind. And now she was also physically moving halfway across the country...

Crumbs, Charity couldn't even find herself a boyfriend, and her envy at the love her sister and Dominic shared made her feel sad, unloved, and unwanted, especially since the only man she'd been attracted to in a very long time had the hots for her sister.

'How did the Halloween party go?' Faith asked, sipping a bright blue cocktail through a straw. 'When I left, it was just getting started.'

'It was a great evening. The kids loved it and I think the parents did, too. Petra was pleased, so that's the main thing.'

Petra worked her socks off to keep the stables solvent, and even though the party had been hard work to arrange, it had been worth it.

'That's good. Did she get you to read a story like she did last year?'

Charity nodded, tucking her long dark hair behind her ears, her mind flitting back to when she'd sat on the bale of hay with the lights low and with Timothy's unwavering gaze caressing her face.

At least, that was what she would have liked to believe. The reality was, he'd more than likely had been imagining it was Faith in front of him, not Charity.

'Did Petra arrange for you to go on another hack with Timothy?' Charity asked, surmising she hadn't when Faith's expression went blank for a moment.

'Timothy? Oh, Harry's brother?' her sister said. 'No, was she supposed to?'

'She said he wanted to go for a ride.'

'She hasn't mentioned anything to me and I'm off to Norwich tomorrow. That's another thing to be sorted – the stables. As things are at the moment, I'm only just managing to fit in my normal duties, and to be honest it's all getting a bit much. I love Midnight to bits, but...'

'...you're not taking him with you,' Charity supplied, her heart plummeting. She'd been anticipating this, but knowing it was coming didn't make it any easier to deal with.

'I still love riding him, you know I do,' Faith continued. 'But I can't take him to Norwich. I can't afford to stable him for one thing, and for another—'

'—you've got other things to occupy you,' Charity finished, sympathetically.

Now that she and Dominic were a couple, Faith's priorities had understandably shifted, but it didn't prevent Charity from feeling upset and strangely hurt. The stables and their horses had been a part of their lives for so long, that Charity couldn't imagine Midnight not being there, or her sister not helping out anymore. They were undeniably drifting apart, even though she knew it was inevitable to a certain extent. She might well feel the same way if she had a lovely boyfriend like Faith had, and an image of Timothy popped into her mind.

She pushed it away.

Faith put her arm around Charity's shoulder and hugged her. 'I can't see Midnight and the stables in my future,' she said. 'Sometimes you have to choose. I've done a lot of soul searching, and I really do think it's time I sold Midnight; even if I wasn't about to move, I can't give him the attention he deserves and it's not fair on him.'

Charity felt like crying. Once upon a time she and Faith had been inseparable, but now their paths were diverging. Faith was ploughing a new furrow, one which didn't involve their once all-encompassing love of horses and riding.

Saddened and upset, Charity couldn't help feeling lost and out of sorts. She was on the cusp of change, and she had an awful feeling she wasn't going to like it.

Timothy girded his loins and walked into the Black Horse. It wasn't as though he was a total stranger to its hop-scented interior because he'd been there before, but Harry had been with him in the past and this evening Timothy was on his own and feeling a little lonely. Harry was with Petra, and Timothy mused that his brother was spending far more time up at the stables than in his rented cottage, so Timothy wouldn't be surprised if Harry moved to Muddypuddle Lane soon.

'A pint of ale, please,' he said, when the landlord asked him what he wanted.

He paid and took a deep draught, then licked his lips, trying to ensure there was no foam left on his beard. He scratched it thoughtfully, debating whether to shave it off. He was still getting used to it, and he couldn't decide whether it suited him.

'How are things. Are you settling in?' the landlord asked, and Timothy rooted around for the man's name.

'I am, thanks, Dave.' Pleased he'd remembered, he tipped his glass at him. 'Can I buy you a drink?'

'That's very kind of you. I'll have it later, if you don't mind. How's that brother of yours?'

'He's good – not that I see a great deal of him.' Timothy might as well be renting the cottage by himself, and he was hoping he'd be able to take over the tenancy if Harry moved in with Petra.

They continued to chat, and as they talked (Dave breaking off to serve now and again), several people smiled at Timothy and nodded, and he realised his face was beginning to be recognised around the village.

At one point when Dave was serving a succession of customers, Timothy turned around to lean his back against the bar, and his gaze wandered around the room as he tried to put names to familiar faces.

When his gaze came to rest on a certain woman he was awfully attracted to, he straightened, then froze. Faith was with someone, and for a second Timothy wondered if his drink had been spiked.

There were **two** of her!

Not believing what he was seeing, he peered at them, resisting the urge to rub his eyes.

Damn, one of them had noticed him, and he saw her nudge the other, so he hastily turned around again as he processed the information.

He hadn't been expecting **that**.

Faith had a twin, and from this distance they looked identical. That might explain things. But the question was, which one of them had he shared his enthusiasm on hearing about his new job with, and was it the same one who had taken him on a hack, or the same one who he'd gazed at like a love-sick teenager during the Halloween party? Because that was the one he wanted to speak to. Or had he been talking to the same one all along?

Unable to decide whether he should speak to them, he ordered another pint instead.

Charity spotted Timothy at the bar long before Faith nudged her in the ribs. She'd seen him walk in looking rather nervous, and she'd noticed how the stiffness of his back and shoulders had gradually eased as he'd taken a deep drink of his pint and began chatting to Dave.

Occasionally he'd glance around and nod at a few people, but she and Faith were sitting in the far corner near the door, and he'd have to turn towards it in order to see them. Charity was quite happy for him to remain oblivious to her presence, especially since she was able to study him (the back of him, at least) to her heart's content.

'There he is, Harry's brother,' Faith hissed. 'See what I mean about him being a dish? Don't look, he's seen us.'

'I thought you wanted me to look?'

'I do, but not when he can see us gawping at him. I don't want him to get the wrong idea. Did I tell you he was very friendly when I took him riding – too friendly, if you ask me.'

'He probably didn't realise you've got a boyfriend,' Charity pointed out. Something was niggling at her and it took her a moment to realise what it was. 'Did you tell him you had a twin?' She'd assumed he knew, because everyone in the village did…but perhaps he didn't.

'I assumed he knew; it didn't occur to me to mention it.'

'I don't think he did know until this evening.' He had done a comical double-take and his eyes had widened. Then he'd turned around as though he was embarrassed.

'Ha! No wonder he looked surprised when he saw us pair sitting here,' Faith chortled.

'I met him when he came for his interview at the vets,' Charity said, her attention still on him. 'He kissed me.'

'**What?** I thought you said you hadn't met him?' Faith turned to her in astonishment. 'There was I telling you what a dish he was, and you'd already snogged him! You kept that quiet.'

'It wasn't like that,' Charity said, and told her what had happened.

'That explains it,' Faith said, finishing her drink. 'He must have thought I was you when we went for the ride. I'd forgotten that used to happen. We don't get it so much anymore. People in Picklewick are used to us and most of them can sort of tell us apart, so they don't get us mixed up.'

'Looks like he did.'

'Does it matter?' Faith asked.

Oh, yes, Charity thought – it mattered a great deal, indeed. But the question was, which twin had caught his eye and which twin did he want to get to know better? 'I quite like him,' she admitted.

'You do?' Faith appeared to be surprised, then a grin spread across her face. 'Are you sure?'

Charity nodded. She was blushing again, and felt all hot and bothered.

 'Why don't you go and talk to him?' Faith suggested.

'I don't think so!' Charity was horrified. She didn't do that kind of thing. Faith was the forward one.

Abruptly Faith rose to her feet. 'I'm off to the loo. Why don't you get a couple more drinks in?'

Charity hesitated. Faith had that look on her face, the one which told Charity she was up to something. Not wanting to go to the bar, she sat there for a while, hoping Faith would return soon and save her the bother. However, it was Charity's turn to buy the drinks and knowing Faith, her sister wouldn't return to their table until Charity had done as she was asked. Faith could be stubborn, especially when she had an agenda. Honestly, Charity thought, this is ridiculous. Would she be as reluctant if Timothy wasn't there? Of course she wouldn't.

She was being silly; Picklewick was a small place and avoiding him would be impossible. She might as well get this over with.

Taking a deep breath, she walked over to the bar and stood next to Timothy, hoping Dave would serve her soon so she could flee back to her seat, mission accomplished.

'Two grapefruit gins, please,' she said, when Dave noticed her. 'One with ice and one without.'

Timothy glanced to his right, spotted her, and gave a start. 'Faith, right?'

'Charity.'

'Where's hope?'

'Ha, ha. We've not heard that before.' Sometimes Charity felt like having stern words with her parents; what on earth had they been thinking?

She watched him process her reply, wondering if he'd be offended, amused, or indifferent, and as he gave her a wide smile, she realised he was none of those things, and she smiled back.

He really did have a lovely smile...

'Are you the nice twin or the evil one?' he asked, and he could have kicked himself as her face fell. She'd seemed so happy to chat with him, too…Embarrassed, he studied the ale in his glass.

'It depends on your perspective,' she retorted. The smile hadn't reappeared, so he wasn't sure if he'd annoyed her or not.

'Do you remember meeting me in the cafe down the road? I sort of, um, kissed you?'

'I remember.'

'Sorry about that. I was so happy and excited I'd got the job, that I had to share it.'

'Would you have shared it as enthusiastically if it had been Amos standing behind you in the queue?'

Timothy pulled a face. 'Probably not.' Then he laughed as the penny dropped. 'Ha! That means you're not Faith.'

'I thought we'd established that.' She was frowning, but she made no move to pick up the drinks she'd paid for and return to her seat.

'What I'm saying is, you didn't accompany me on the ride last week.'

'No, that was my sister.'

It felt odd that he'd thought her name was Faith when her real name was Charity all along. It was nice. It suited her – softer, somehow. But at least it explained why the woman who had taken him on the ride hadn't recognised him.

'And which one of you was at the Halloween party at the stables?' he asked.

'We both were, but Faith left early to meet her boyfriend.'

He felt she was trying to tell him something; that Faith was out of bounds, perhaps? He didn't care, it was Charity he was interested in. More than interested...

There was Faith now, walking towards them, and he felt deflated that Charity would go back to her table. He would like nothing better than for her to stay at the bar and keep him company.

The two women were incredibly alike he thought, inspecting them whilst trying not to let either of them see. Apart, he'd most definitely have trouble knowing one from the other – it would be a fifty-fifty guess, but when they were standing next to each other as they were doing now, he noticed subtle differences. The main one was that Charity appeared more reserved than her sister. However, there was a way of telling them apart when they weren't together, he saw – Charity had a small scar on her cheek, and he filed the information away for future reference.

He also now knew which twin it was he'd been staring longingly at during the

Halloween party, and he was relieved to discover it had been Charity.

He watched Faith lean in close, cup her hand around Charity's ear and whisper, and he noticed how Charity looked panicked for a moment, before she inhaled and nodded.

To his surprise, Faith sauntered towards the door, swinging her bag and waving goodbye, leaving her sister at the bar.

He waited for Charity to gather herself before he asked, 'Is your sister coming back?'

She bit her lip and shook her head.

'I'd offer to buy you a drink, but you already have two in front of you and I don't want you to think I'm trying to get you drunk,' he joked, but when he failed to elicit a response he said, 'I'm going to sit down. Would you care to join me?'

She narrowed her eyes, then appeared to come to a decision as she picked up both drinks and made her way to the table she'd not long vacated.

Timothy sat next to her, in the same seat her sister had. He put his drink down and prepared to do battle. He had a feeling it was going to take more than his usual charm to break down Charity's barriers, and he very much wanted to get to know her better.

'How long have you worked in the care home?' he asked, and was gratified to see she was pleased he remembered.

And as she told him, and they began to discover more about each other, Timothy realised that for the first time in his life he was smitten. It was a rather pleasant sensation, and he was disappointed when Dave announced last orders a couple of hours later.

'Gosh, is that the time?' she said. 'I have to go – I've got an early start in the morning.'

He drained what was left in his glass and stood up, and the two of them made their way to the door, but once outside, he felt at a loss. 'I'll walk you home,' he offered, assuming she lived close enough to walk. She certainly hadn't driven to the pub and she wasn't making any move to order a taxi.

Her smile was shy. 'I only live around the corner.'

'I'd like to make sure you get home okay, if that's all right with you?'

'If you're sure. I live in the opposite direction to Harry's cottage.'

Timothy wouldn't have cared if she lived at the North Pole. 'It's no bother,' he assured her.

They fell into step side-by-side, and he felt his heart race as her arm brushed against his. It seemed only natural he should reach for her hand.

He felt Charity begin to pull away, but then her fingers curled around his and his stomach somersaulted with desire. Her hand was soft and warm, snuggling into his like a baby rabbit. Actually, that was what she reminded him of, a shy, nervous bunny. It made him feel all protective and masculine.

Walking in silence, Timothy cast about for something to say, before realising there was no need to say anything. He was perfectly content to stroll along the quiet streets of Picklewick without needing to talk.

'This is me,' she said quietly, as they halted outside a terraced cottage.

Suddenly, he felt awkward and uncertain. He so badly wanted to kiss her, but he couldn't tell whether she'd be amenable or not.

Should he ask her? Or would he look a prat?

He'd ask her.

Timothy became aware of Charity gazing at him with a bemused expression, and he also became aware he was still holding her hand.

'Can I kiss you?' he blurted.

Her eyes shone luminously in the streetlights, and she paused for such a long time he was convinced she was going to say no. But finally she nodded and, still clasping her hand, he dipped his head towards her.

She lifted her chin as he brought his mouth down to hers, her pupils large and dark as she locked her gaze on him. As their lips met and he felt her soft breath on his face, her eyelids fluttered closed and she let out a soft sigh.

Tentative at first, he kissed her gently, delicately, feather-light in his delight. But as she responded and her mouth opened, passion sparked through his body and he had to hold himself back for fear of scaring her with his urgency.

He deepened the kiss, then eased slowly away. He was breathing hard and his heart pounded, and he'd never felt so lost in a woman as he had just now. It was exhilarating and frightening at the same time.

Slowly, tantalisingly, Charity opened her eyes, her expression unfathomable. Wanting to kiss her again, Timothy held back. It might be a good idea to give himself some time to reflect on what had just happened before he risked further physical contact.

'Have you got any plans for tomorrow?' he asked. His voice was gruff, and he cleared his throat.

'I'm in work until four.'

'What about the evening?' He felt on safer ground now, as his pulse dropped to more normal levels and his unruly emotions were brought under control.

'Bonfire Night. There's a display in the park. It's only a small one.' She seemed as flustered as he was.

'Oh, yes, I'd forgotten about that.'

'There'll be hotdogs and toffee apples. You should go.'

Timothy frowned. Fireworks weren't Harry's thing and Timothy didn't want to go on his own. 'I might,' he said, doubtfully.

'Okay, I might see you there, then.'

'Would you like to go with me?' he blurted.

'I'd love to. My sister and I usually go together, but she's off to Norwich tomorrow.'

'So you'll settle for accompanying me instead?' His tone was wry.

Charity laughed and the atmosphere lightened a degree or two, although the kiss they'd shared continued to hover in the air between them. 'I'll meet you by the hotdog stand – six-thirty?'

Timothy didn't think about what he was going to say next, until he'd said it. 'We can go for a drink afterwards, if you like.'

Her shy smile and the way she peeped up at him from underneath her lashes told him that she **would** like.

'Can I have your phone number?' he asked and when she gave it to him, he immediately rang her. 'There, now you've got mine, too. I'll see you tomorrow.' He trailed a finger down her cheek, then cupped her face. 'Nice meeting you properly,' he said.

As he walked away, heading for home, he felt her gaze on his back. It was a wonderfully pleasant sensation.

Timothy slumped onto the sofa, a glass of water in his hand. He hadn't bothered to turn the telly on even though he was too wired to go to bed yet. His mind swirled with thoughts of Charity, and he couldn't stop smiling. Every now and again he'd chuckle when he recalled turning around, seeing a double image of Faith, and wondering if his drink had been spiked.

When he thought about that glorious kiss, his heart missed a beat. He had never felt this way about a girl before. It was so new to him and he couldn't wait to see her again.

The sound of the front door opening made him jump and in turn Harry let out a yell when he saw Timothy.

'Why are you sitting in the dark?' his brother cried, turning on a sidelight. 'You nearly gave me a heart attack.'

'I didn't expect you home tonight,' Timothy said.

'Petra had to come into the village to pick Amos up from the pub, so I thought I'd sleep in my own bed for a change considering I've got to be up and out at the crack of dawn tomorrow.'

Timothy remembered Harry saying something about promising to visit a stable several miles away, where three of their mounts had lost shoes, and who were all due to be ridden tomorrow. Harry tried not to work weekends, unlike

Timothy who was frequently on call, but this was an exception.

Not for the first time Timothy wondered if he was cramping Harry's style by moving in with him. With Amos, Petra's uncle, living at the stables, Timothy suspected Harry and Petra used to spend time at the cottage in order to be alone. However, that was now denied them, because of him.

'I might look for somewhere to rent soon,' he said. 'You and Petra need a place you can be together.'

Harry yawned and stretched, his fingers touching the living room ceiling. 'This isn't it,' Harry said. 'She would never spend the night at the cottage – it's too far away from her horses.'

'But if you ever want me to make myself scarce, just say.'

'By the moony look on your face, it's me who should be making myself scarce.'

'I've not got a moony look on my face.'

'Yes, you have.' Harry smirked. 'Is it anything to do with Charity Jones?'

'I don't know what you mean,' Timothy retorted, loftily.

'You were with her most of the evening.'

'How do you know that?'

'Amos. He was in the snug playing darts. He saw you together and said you looked like a fella who'd lost a penny and found a pound.'

Amos was right – that was exactly how he felt!

For once Faith wasn't spending the night at Dominic's place, wanting to be at home for her last night in Picklewick for a couple of weeks, and when Charity crept into the house expecting everyone to be in bed, she discovered her sister had waited up for her.

'Well?' Faith demanded, as soon as Charity cleansed her face and slipped into her pyjamas. Faith was already snuggled up in Charity's bed, and she scooted over to make room for her.

'Well, what?' Charity feigned ignorance, but when Faith whacked her with a pillow, she couldn't stop the huge smile spreading across her face.

'Are you seeing him again?' Faith wanted to know, and Charity nodded.

'I'm meeting him at the firework display tomorrow.'

'Go, you! You like him a lot, don't you?'

Charity was thankful it was dark so Faith couldn't see her blush, but her sister knew her only too well.

'I'm pleased for you,' Faith continued. 'It's about time you had some love in your life, so don't be embarrassed. From the little I saw, he seemed to be into you, too.'

Charity certainly hoped he was.

'Did you see his face when he realised there are two of us?' Faith chortled. 'I'd forgotten how much fun it was.'

'No, you can't play a trick on him,' Charity warned, knowing what her sister was like. It had been her favourite thing to do when they were younger.

'Spoilsport.' Faith dragged the duvet over her. Charity dragged it back. 'Did you kiss?' Faith asked, and when Charity failed to answer, she cried, 'You did! You kissed him. What was it like? Is he a good kisser? Were there tongues?'

'**Faith!**' Charity and her sister had always shared everything (almost everything – things had changed since Dominic had arrived on the scene) but Charity wanted to keep the details of their kiss to herself.

It was too precious to be shared.

And she did keep it to herself, bringing it out only when Faith had retired to her own bed, leaving Charity alone with her thoughts and her dreams.

She'd had boyfriends before but none she'd felt such a strong attraction to, and it had nothing to do with Timothy being so good looking. It ran much deeper. She knew it was daft and far too soon to be thinking like this (they hardly knew each other) but she felt as though she'd known him forever.

When she finally drifted off to sleep, it was with his image in her mind and the taste of him on her lips.

CHAPTER SIX

Charity was still in bed when she heard Faith get up, and she rolled over for an extra five minutes of blissful snoozing. Eventually though, she had to force her reluctant body out of bed and get ready for work. Tired didn't begin to describe how she felt this morning; she was exhausted from having a fitful restless night. And every time she'd woken, Timothy's face had swanned into her mind and had refused to budge.

She kept seeing his smile, the way his mouth twisted slightly unevenly giving him a wickedly sexy air, the single frown line between his eyes when he was concentrating on something she'd said, hearing his infectious laugh... She also kept reliving the moment when his lips had touched hers, and the cascade of emotions that had poured through her and the way her heart had stuttered made the blood sing in her veins.

After visiting the stables extremely early this morning, coming back in time to wave Faith off and make her promise to message her as soon as she got to Norwich, Charity made her way into work, her thoughts about Timothy interspersed with her worry about the stables. She couldn't stop thinking about Faith having to sell Midnight. Her sister had owned the horse since she was fourteen and he was six. It was a long time, especially in equine years, but Charity knew deep down that Faith wasn't being fair to him, even if she didn't intend to leave Picklewick. He needed to be ridden far more frequently than Faith could manage. He was a big lad and spirited, so was totally unsuitable for the vast majority of riders at the stables. Petra took him out now and again, but she had her own horse, Hercules, who needed to be exercised. Charity rode Storm, wanting to ensure her horse was fit, so that only left Harry, who sometimes saddled up and went for a ride, or Nathan, who was the stable's handyman. Nathan occasionally accompanied Petra on a ride, and Charity had gone out with him once or twice. But Midnight still didn't have enough exercise, and he was starting to become a little unruly.

Maybe Timothy could ride him, Charity mused, but that didn't address the issue of the arrangement the twins had with Petra; both horses were liveried for free in exchange for the sisters' help around the stables. Over the past few months Charity had found herself picking up some of Faith's slack, and she'd been fine with that – all that mattered to Charity was that Faith was happy. But Charity simply didn't have the time to ride both horses herself, as well as doing everything else.

As usual, Charity stowed her coat and bag in the staffroom, said hello to Rose who was the office administrator, and spoke to a few of the residents before she began work. Most of them were either still in bed, or were in the process of getting up, which could be a long-drawn-out affair for some of them, involving a couple of staff members and a hoist.

Charity could smell bacon, and her stomach growled. Honeymead Care Home lived up to its name, in that it cared for its residents very well indeed, and the food it provided was no exception. There was always a decent range on offer for breakfast, and Charity would have loved to eat a bacon sandwich right now, having skipped breakfast.

'Smells nice, doesn't it?' Olive said, as she tottered past. 'Want me to save you a slice?'

Charity gave the air a final sniff. 'That's very kind of you, Olive, but I've already eaten,' she lied, not wanting to give the old lady any excuse to smuggle food out of the dining room. She was a bit of a madam for stuffing half of what was on her plate into her pockets. Lena, Olive's daughter, was worried that hoarding food might be a sign of dementia, especially as the care home offered three substantial meals, plus home-made cakes, crisps and biscuits in the cafe area for residents to help themselves.

Charity knew the reason for Olive's penchant for secreting food about her person, but Olive had sworn her to secrecy. She was feeding a stray cat, who lingered in the garden outside her room every morning and evening. Charity wasn't convinced cats liked roast potatoes, though.

'Do you need me to bring in any more cat food?' Charity asked.

'I've still got some, but I've had to put it in the safe,' Olive said. 'I don't want anyone to find it, you see. They might ask questions.'

Charity shook her head. 'The safe is for your valuables,' she reminded her. Every resident had their own safe in their rooms, much like a hotel room.

'That's okay,' Olive said cheerfully. 'I haven't got any.'

At least if Olive was feeding the cat proper food, then she wasn't smuggling half a roast dinner out of the dining room, and Lena wouldn't worry about her mother as much.

'You look tired, my girl,' Olive said, waving her walking stick at her. 'Have you been out partying?'

'I don't like parties, although I am going to watch the fireworks tonight. You should have a good view of them from the terrace.'

'Bah, noisy things. I like the colours though, so perhaps I'll watch from inside. Do you have a nice young man to accompany you?'

Charity smiled. 'I think I do. It's the new vet.'

'Ooh, a new vet? Do you think he'll take a look at Marigold?'

'Marigold?'

'The cat.'

'I thought his name was Rambo?'

'That was when I thought he was a him. Now I think she's a her.'

'I see. I can ask him. She might be a bit difficult to catch, if she's semi-wild.'

'What's this fella of yours like? Is he handsome?'

Charity nibbled on her bottom lip. 'I think so.'

'Does he treat you well?'

'Tonight will be our first proper date. He walked me home from the pub last night, though,' she confided.

'I wish I was your age, and knew what I know now,' Olive said. 'If you like him, don't hang about. And make sure he puts a ring on it. That girl on tv, the one who shakes her tail feathers, has got it right.'

'Beyonce?'

'That's the one. Marvin took three years to propose to me. I was getting jolly fed up, I can tell you.'

'It's too soon to think about that,' Charity said, relieved when the main door buzzed and she had to hurry away to let someone in, leaving Olive to make her way into the dining room.

It was Lena, Olive's daughter.

'Your mum is about to have her breakfast,' Charity informed her. 'Why don't you have a coffee while you wait?'

'Good idea,' the woman said, and Charity had no sooner made one for her and one for herself, when the door buzzed again.

This time it was Amos, and he'd brought Petra's black Cocker Spaniel with him.

'That's so kind of you to bring Queenie,' Charity said. 'Brian especially, will love to see her. He misses his dog dreadfully. Take a seat and I'll make you a hot drink, then I'll tell Brian you're here.'

'Thanks, my lovely,' Amos said, easing himself into the chair next to Lena, who was fussing over Queenie. The dog was lapping up the attention. 'I'll have a tea, if you don't mind. I saw you and Timothy in the Black Horse last night. The pair of you looked quite cosy.'

'Would Timothy be the new vet?' Lena asked, scruffling Queenie's silky ears.

'It would. Nice lad is Harry's brother,' Amos said.

'Harry's nice, too,' Lena said. 'How is he getting on with Petra? Any sign of wedding bells?'

Charity left them to chat and retreated to her desk. What was this fascination with marriage today, she wondered. It was all anyone seemed able to talk about. There was more to life than getting wed, although she strongly suspected her sister didn't think so, and once again Charity felt the breeze of change blow through her mind.

But this time, it carried an image of Timothy with it.

Timothy, shirt off, lathered up his hands and forearms using antibacterial soap, and prepared to do battle. His opponent was a cow who was having difficulty calving, and he knew the next half an hour or so wasn't going to be pretty. It would be dirty, strenuous, and hard work, and was definitely the less glamorous side of being a vet. But hopefully, there would be a healthy mother and baby at the end of it.

As he put on a plastic apron and donned a pair of arm-length plastic gloves, Timothy was in his element. He preferred horses, but a vet in a general practice couldn't choose his clients. If an animal was in trouble it needed to be helped, and this poor creature wouldn't be able to give birth without assistance.

Grimacing, he examined her. 'I can feel a leg and a nose,' he said to the farmer. 'Hand me the calving rope, I'm going to have to bring the other leg forward before I can pull the calf out.'

It was a good half an hour before he was finally able to stand back and watch the new mum lick her black and white calf clean.

'He's a decent size,' the farmer said happily, as Timothy stripped off the plastic apron and gloves, and gave himself another wash.

Calving was a mucky business.

'He certainly is,' he agreed, satisfied he'd done a good job. He loved assisting at births when there was a good outcome, and he smiled as the baby shook his head and blinked. In a few minutes it would struggle unsteadily to its feet and take its first drink of milk. Timothy would wait until that happened, then he'd make his way to his next client.

Suitably dressed again, he put his things away and tidied up after himself.

'Settling in all right?' the farmer asked. 'Brandon told me he had a new vet on his staff.'

Timothy nodded – he was settling in just fine, and with each passing day he felt more at home. He'd made the right decision in moving to Picklewick. He enjoyed working at the practice, and he loved living in the village. Harry didn't seem to mind having him around, so that was a bonus, but he still intended to get his own place eventually. He'd have to save a bit first for a deposit, unless...?

He and Harry owned the house in Cheltenham between them, having inherited it when their parents died. What if they were to sell it? Timothy had put it in the hands of a letting agent so it was bringing in some income for the pair of them, but he guessed Harry had no intention of ever living in it again, and now Timothy had left he didn't believe he would return to the family home either. Picklewick was a fresh start for both of them.

Timothy said goodbye to the farmer, plugged his next client's address into the Satnav and trundled off up the track, wincing at each pothole. Relieved to reach the tarmac road, he pulled onto it and was soon on his way, letting the soothing electronic voice guide him as his thoughts turned to fresh starts and new beginnings. He hoped one of those new beginnings would involve Charity. She'd managed to get under his skin, which was a first, and he was astonished at how much he was looking forward to seeing her again. He couldn't wait for this evening, although he wasn't entirely sure whether it was a date or not.

What he was sure about though, was his desire to kiss her again, and to keep kissing her until she'd fallen for him as deeply as he'd managed to fall for her.

'I hate Bonfire Night,' Petra muttered for the tenth time. She said the same thing every year, and for good reason. Horses, like most animals, hated sudden loud noises, and there had been whistling explosions for the past few days as people set off the odd rocket or two prematurely. The fireworks had been known to go on for days afterwards, too. 'Sodding fireworks,' she added, sourly.

Charity understood where Petra was coming from, because even with the stables being so far out of the village, the noise of the fireworks carried, and the official display would be twenty minutes of incessant loud noise and lights in the sky. The horses would absolutely hate it, which was why Charity had popped up to the stables immediately after work to help Petra bed them down for the night.

At least if they were in their stalls before the madness began, they would be less likely to panic and injure themselves. And, of course, Petra would be there to reassure them.

On the other hand, Charity loved Bonfire Night and always had done. The smell of woodsmoke from the bonfire itself, the scent of cordite (was it? she was never sure), the sparklers, the lights illuminating the sky for the briefest of moments, then falling back to earth...the whole thing was magical and catapulted her firmly back to her childhood. Then there was the huge bonfire, and the astonishing heat which radiated from it, the hotdog and burger stands with the delicious aroma of frying onions. And tonight there would be the added excitement of seeing Timothy again.

Last night had been wonderful. They'd talked for ages, and it was as though she'd been speaking to an old friend. She had so much to learn about him, yet she felt like she'd known him her whole life. It was a most extraordinary thing.

Then they had kissed and her world had shrunk to that incredibly wonderful meeting of their lips and the sensations swirling through her.

'Charity?'

'Huh?'

'You were miles away,' Petra said. 'In a proper daydream you were. Would that lovesick look on your face have anything to do with Harry's brother, by any chance?'

Good lord, did everyone in Picklewick know her business? Petra normally didn't bother with matters of the heart, but she was certainly taking an active interest in Charity's love life.

'No comment,' she replied haughtily, and stuck her nose in the air.

Petra was right though, Charity **was** all dreamy.

She couldn't stop thinking about Timothy, and she hugged herself in delight.

She was falling for him, and it felt absolutely wonderful.

CHAPTER SEVEN

Timothy sniffed the air appreciatively, the aroma of fried onions bringing back memories of half-forgotten Bonfire Nights from his childhood. Times like this were bitter-sweet, as he remembered being taken to the display in Cheltenham by his parents. After they'd died, Harry had gone with him, but Timothy had quickly grown out of being escorted by an adult (which Harry was, as his legal guardian) and preferred to go with his friends instead.

Picklewick's Bonfire Night celebrations were an altogether smaller affair and as he walked through the crowd searching for Charity, he saw many familiar faces. He might not be able to put names to them all, but nods and smiles were exchanged, and occasionally he was stopped by someone whose animal he had treated and he had a quick chat.

The bonfire hadn't been lit yet – apparently that would happen after the fireworks – and most people were gathered behind a line of barriers, beyond which shadowy figures carrying torches could be seen doing last minute checks.

Timothy stopped and scanned the field, his gaze flitting over faces, seeking out one in particular. Then he spotted her near the hotdog stand, talking to an older woman, who he guessed might be her mum as the two women shared similar features.

Hastening over, he came to a halt in front of Charity and smiled broadly. Gosh, was she a sight for sore eyes! She wore a bobble hat which framed her face, and was bundled up in a scarf and a thick winter coat, and had sturdy boots on her feet. Her breath misted the air and as she blew on her hands his gaze came to rest on her puckered lips and he longed to kiss them.

'Hi,' he said, shuffling from foot to foot, feeling absurdly nervous, before turning his attention to the woman next to her. 'Hello.'

The woman held out her hand. 'You must be Timothy, the new vet. Pleased to meet you. I'm Valerie, Charity's mum.'

He shook her hand, conscious of her scrutiny of him, and he hoped she approved of what she saw. 'Pleased to meet you too,' he said.

She held his gaze for a moment, then said to Charity, 'I'll go and find your father. No doubt he's near the beer tent. I just hope he's not got his hands on any sparklers. He nearly set his hair on fire last year,' Valerie told Timothy, with an eye roll and a deep sigh.

Charity watched her mother leave, her eyes warm and soft. 'It might not seem like it, but they love each other to bits,' she said. 'They are my benchmark – I want to have a marriage like that one day.'

An image of his own parents drifted into his mind. They'd been happy and he wondered, as he often did, what they would have been like now if they'd lived. And what would Harry's life have been like? Vastly different without having his younger brother to take care of, Timothy knew. He'd have become a vet, for one thing. But Timothy recognised that Harry was happy now. He had a job he loved and a woman he loved even more. Harry seemed more settled and contented than Timothy could remember him ever being, and he was so pleased for him.

Timothy was also happy, and he'd be happier still if the woman by his side was to become his girlfriend. To test the water and to make sure last night wasn't a one-off, he put his arms around her, gratified when she lifted her chin for a kiss.

He kept it brief, mindful her parents were nearby and there were loads of children around, but the taste of her made his heart race, and her perfume had his head spinning with longing; and after he'd pulled away he was desperate to kiss her again.

He had no idea what was happening to him, or how to make sense of the emotions surging through his mind and his body, but he knew he liked it. He liked it very much indeed.

Charity would have been happy for the kiss to have gone on all evening, but they were in a very public place and her parents were close by; she didn't want them to have to witness her snogging the face off the new vet.

Giggling, she wondered how long people would continue to refer to Timothy as the "new vet". Years, probably.

'What are you laughing at?' he asked her, dropping a swift kiss onto the end of her cold nose. His lips were incredibly warm, and she glowed at his touch.

When she told him, he laughed. 'Probably until Tina and Brandon employ another vet,' he said. 'Then I'll become the "not-so-new" vet.'

He was about to say something else but a blast of music drowned him out, and she realised the firework display was about to start, so she caught hold of his hand and dragged him over to the barriers. Charity would have liked to continue to hold Timothy's hand, but he pushed her forward into a space, and took up position behind her. She hoped he'd be able to see over the top of her head, but as for herself she didn't care about watching the fireworks. All she could concentrate on was the man standing behind her. He was so close she could feel the solidity of his chest against her back, and she shivered with the anticipation of being kissed again later.

Possibly thinking her shiver was from the cold, he wrapped his arms around her and pulled her into him, his mouth near to her ear. She wished he'd nibble it, so she tilted her head slightly to the side, feeling incredibly brazen. His breath fanned her cheek, and she snuggled deeper into him as his arms tightened around her.

They stayed that way all through the display, their faces lifted to the sky as they became immersed in the lightshow overhead. And when it was over, he kissed the skin below her ear, and she shivered again as a tingle of desire shot through her.

'Shall we warm ourselves by the bonfire?' he asked.

Charity felt hot enough already. Any additional heating might result in her bursting into flames. However, she was happy to wander over to the pyre and feel the warmth on her face and sniff the aromatic smell of burning wood. The crackle of flames and the snap of burning branches replaced the music which had played during the display, and gradually people began to make their way home, many of them with sleepy children in tow.

Content to stand and watch the flames, the flickering light casting dancing shadows across the grass, Charity uttered a deep sigh of happiness. The night was perfect – a clear sky, an autumn chill to the air, velvety darkness beyond the reach of the light from the fire – and she was spending it with a man she felt a strong attraction to, who was just as attracted to her if the passion in his kisses was any indication. Beneath the building excitement they generated in her was a euphoria she hadn't experienced before, and during one of their subdued clinches she'd caught herself fast-forwarding several years to marriage, a home of their own, and a baby in a nursery.

Laughing inside at herself (she'd even tried out Charity Milton in her head, to see how it sounded), she was brought back to the present with a jolt when she heard her mother's voice.

'There you are!' Valerie exclaimed, as she walked towards them, hand-in-hand with Charity's dad. It was so cute the way they still held hands after all these years, Charity thought.

Charity beamed at her parents then introduced Timothy to her father. The poor guy, she thought – he'd already met her parents and he wasn't even her boyfriend yet. However, in a village like Picklewick it was hard not to get to know everyone, so she supposed it was going to happen sooner rather than later.

After the two men had been introduced and had found some common ground discussing sport (with an eyeroll from Valerie), Charity linked arms with her mum as they strolled across the field and into the village.

'How is it going with Timothy?' her mother asked. 'You seem very loved up.'

'He's gorgeous,' Charity murmured, not wanting to risk Timothy overhearing.

'I'm so pleased for you.' Valerie gave her arm a squeeze.

'Don't go putting the cart before the horse,' Charity warned. 'Technically, this is only our first date. He hasn't even mentioned seeing me again.'

'He will.' Her mum sounded positive. She stopped walking to allow the others to catch up, and said, 'I wonder if Timothy would like to come to lunch tomorrow? Your dad has bought the most enormous chicken – I don't know how we're going to fit it in the oven, let alone eat it all. We're going to need some help.'

Charity noticed Timothy's shocked expression out of the corner of her eye, and she hoped her mum wasn't putting him in an awkward position.

Oh dear, it had all been going so well until now...

'I'd love to, Mrs Jones,' Timothy replied, delighted to have been asked, but concerned what Charity might think of the invitation. 'I'm going to have to decline though, because I might have to dart off. I'm on call, you see.'

Mrs Jones looked at her daughter and then back at him. 'It's perfectly fine,' she said. 'We don't mind, and I have a feeling Charity might have to get used to you

being on call. Please call me Valerie –
Mrs Jones is so formal.'

Timothy had been planning on shoving a
pizza in the oven. He had an open
invitation to eat at the stables (Amos did
most of the cooking and was rather good
at it), but he didn't want to intrude on
Harry and Petra. Harry didn't need his
little brother hanging about, especially
when he had a girlfriend.

On glancing at Charity to make sure she
was happy with the situation, he was
thrilled to see she was beaming.

'In that case, I'd be delighted,' he said.

'Alan, let's leave these love birds to it,'
Valerie said to her husband, and moved
away leaving him and Charity standing on
the pavement.

'It's still early,' Timothy said. 'Fancy going
to the pub?' He didn't really want a drink,
but neither did he want to say goodnight.

She sighed heavily. 'I'd suggest you came back to mine for a coffee, but I still live at home.'

'Harry is at the stables, so how about a nightcap at my place?' His heart was thumping at the thought of the two of them being alone.

He had no intention of dragging her off to bed (although he would like nothing better than to make love to her) but being able to kiss her whilst sitting on a comfy sofa in a warm room would be something of a novelty; and he was acutely aware of how new this relationship of theirs was.

There were so many firsts ahead of them and he wanted to savour every single one. Which was exactly what he did, as the coffee he'd made sat untouched on the side table, for the next hour of delicious kissing and cuddling. And when he escorted her home, anxious not to let her out of his sight any sooner than he absolutely had to, his heart sang and he was so happy he wanted to tell the whole world.

'I had a great time,' he said when they reached her house, and he turned to kiss her again. He couldn't get enough of those delectable lips.

'So did I. Are you sure you want to come to lunch tomorrow? You don't have to.'

'Don't you want me to?'

'That's not what I said.' She dropped her gaze. 'It's not easy getting to know someone, is it?'

He placed a finger under her chin and raised her head. 'No, but it's good fun, and I want to get to know you an awful lot better. I want to know you inside and out, even if it takes me a lifetime to do it.'

Charity giggled softly. She sounded nervous.

'Too fast?' he asked.

'Just a little.'

'We can take things as slowly as you want.'

'This is only our first proper date,' she pointed out.

'I know, and I've loved every second of it.'

'Me, too.' She looked away, and he realised this was as new to her as it was to him.

'Until tomorrow.' He kissed her again. It lasted quite some time. If it was up to him, it would have lasted all night, and then some.

Finally, he released her, although she seemed as reluctant as he to end the embrace, and he knew he was utterly smitten. It might be early days and they'd hardly known each other long, but he was looking forward to seeing where their relationship would lead.

As he dawdled home, an image of Harry entered his mind and he fervently hoped he would find with Charity what Harry had found with Petra.

If the loss of his parents had taught him one thing, it was that life was incredibly short and love was all that ultimately mattered.

'You're back then? I was about to send out a search party,' Valerie joked.

'Very funny. Not.' Charity slung her coat on the back of a chair and took her hat and scarf off.

'Oi, put that away,' her mother instructed.

'I was going to.' Crumbs, living at home could be a trial sometimes. She adored her parents but they continued to treat her like a kid, and if she was honest she continued to act like one on occasion. She'd noticed Faith was the same when she was at home, and Charity thought back to the peace and solitude of Timothy's house.

He was in the same boat to a certain extent, because he was sharing a house with his brother who was also a father figure. It must have been dreadful for them both when their parents died she thought, her heart going out to the brothers. Timothy had told her the story, and she'd heard the grief in his voice and had sensed a deep well of sadness in him, which she guessed would always be there. It made her own heart ache for him, and she would have loved nothing more than to be able to ease his pain.

She hung her coat up in the cupboard under the stairs and put her hat and scarf away, then slumped onto the sofa.

'Did you enjoy the fireworks?' Valerie asked.

'Hmm.' Charity knew what her mum was fishing for, and it had nothing to do with the fireworks in the sky and everything to do with the fireworks in her chest. Her heart kept skipping a beat and her tummy turned over each time she thought of Timothy – which was every other second. He was so gorgeous—

'You didn't mind me asking him to lunch, did you?' Her mother broke into her thoughts, and Charity wished she'd gone straight to bed and avoided the third-degree questioning which she simply knew she was about to be subjected to.

'Not at all,' she replied. 'It was kind of you to invite him.'

'I've been thinking about Faith and Dominic...' Valerie said. She looked wistful.

'What about them?' Charity was thankful the conversation was moving away from her and Timothy.

'I wouldn't be surprised if there are wedding bells in the next year or so.'

The very same thing had occurred to Charity. It was a scary thought. Throughout their lives, the twins had relied on each other first and foremost – parents, friends and boyfriends had always had second billing. Then Dominic had arrived on the scene and things had slowly changed. It was only natural for Faith's priority to be the man she loved, but Charity had felt hurt, all the same.

Now, though, she felt a glimmer of what Faith must be feeling, and a new understanding of what her sister was going through crept into Charity's mind.

One day, Charity herself might feel the same way about someone. She sincerely hoped so.

Maybe that man would be Timothy?

Timothy's mouth was watering as soon as he walked into the hall of the Jones's house the following day, as the glorious aroma of roasting chicken assaulted his nose.

'Smells nice,' he said, sniffing appreciatively.

Charity's arms snaked around his neck, and he dipped his head towards her.

'So do you,' he added, then he kissed her, wishing he didn't have to stop.

'Come into the living room,' she said. 'Drink?' She showed him into a spacious room with two large sofas and a set of patio doors leading out to a generous garden. It was empty, but he heard noises coming from the kitchen so he assumed her parents were in there.

'A soft one, please. I'm on call, don't forget.'

She fetched him a cold drink from the kitchen, then sat next to him.

He felt rather awkward and Charity smiling nervously at him didn't help, so he decided to try to break the tension.

Leaning in close, he whispered in her ear, 'Do they bite?'

She giggled and any inhibitions dissipated. 'Only on weekdays,' she whispered back.

'What are you two whispering about?' Valerie asked, appearing in the doorway. 'Hi, Timothy, how are you?'

Timothy made small talk whilst helping Charity lay the table, and as he did so he felt as though he was getting to know a little more about Charity herself. He could see where her personality came from –

her dad was quiet and reserved, her mum was far more lively and talkative. Her parents were opposites and she seemed to follow her father.

Come to think of it, he and Charity were opposites too, Timothy thought. He had always been up for a laugh and ready for fun, most of it noisy and exuberant. He was much more outgoing than Charity, he realised. Maybe it was part of the attraction between them – she was ying and he was yang. Or the other way around. Whatever...they fitted together as though they were two halves of the same person. Like Charity and Faith. Like Valerie and Alan.

There was a gentle, easy atmosphere between Charity and her parents, and a stab of pain caught him in the chest. Would his parents have been like this with him? Would they have welcomed Charity as warmly as Valerie and Alan had welcomed him? He was certain they would have done, and he felt their loss more keenly than usual.

 Timothy had just finished the last morsel of chicken, having used it to mop up the smidge of gravy on his plate, and had placed his knife and fork down with a replete sigh, when his phone rang.

Taking it out of his pocket, he smiled apologetically. 'Sorry, I'll have to take this,' he said, and got to his feet.

His heart sank when he discovered he had a patient to see to. After promising to be there as soon as possible, he returned to the dining room to deliver the news.

'I've got to go,' he said. 'Thank you so much for inviting me. It was absolutely delicious.' He turned to Charity. 'Sorry,' he said. 'I'll give you a ring later?'

'You'd better had.' She got up and accompanied him to the door.

'Hopefully this won't take long,' he said, mentally crossing his fingers, and he bent his head to kiss her.

His joy when she slipped her arm around his neck and pulled her down to him, was only tempered by the knowledge that her parents might hear and could probably guess what they were doing. But as he left, he felt a warm glow of happiness which kept him going throughout the rest of the afternoon.

Charity dashed to the door when she heard the bell ring later that evening and opened it to find Timothy hiding behind a bunch of flowers.

'These are for your mum,' he said. 'To say thank you. Do you think she'll mind I bought them from the garage? The supermarket wasn't open.'

'She'll be thrilled you even thought of it,' Charity said. 'Come in and you can give them to her yourself.'

'Oh, you shouldn't have!' Valerie exclaimed as soon as she saw them, and she buried her nose in the colourful petals, inhaling deeply. She ran some water into the sink and popped the flowers into it. 'I've got a vase around here somewhere,' she muttered, opening and closing cupboards. She stopped searching and turned to him. 'Would you like a cup of tea?'

Charity leapt in before he had a chance to say a word. 'Thanks, Mum, but if it's okay with you, we'll nip to the pub for an hour or so.' Lunch had been lovely, but she wanted Timothy all to herself, and even the thought of having to put up with the other customers was better than sitting there with her mum and dad, being subjected to their knowing looks. Her mum hadn't stopped talking about how nice Timothy was, and dropping not-so-subtle hints that he was a keeper.

'Was your call-out okay?' she asked, as she pulled her front door closed behind them, and took hold of his hand. It seemed like the most perfectly natural thing to do, and she relished the feel of his palm on hers.

'Not really. A sheep had been worried by a dog. I stitched her up, but I doubt she'll last the night.'

She listened sympathetically. It wasn't easy losing an animal. She'd witnessed a fair few losses at the stables, from chickens to a cat, and on one awful occasion an old horse that had been put out to pasture years ago but who Petra still loved and cared for had died suddenly in the field.

'What was that?' she cried, when a loud bang made her shriek and set her heart racing. Timothy jumped too, and let out a cry.

'Dear god!' he exclaimed. 'Someone is setting off their own fireworks. Sales of them to individuals should be banned.' He grimaced. 'I sound like a right old fogey,' he said, 'but people don't realise how much distress they cause to animals. Harry was saying that Queenie spent most of Bonfire Night hiding under the stairs, and the stables are a fair distance away from the village.'

'I hope Storm is okay.' Charity chewed on her lip, imagining how scared her horse must be at the loud noises. And poor Queenie – the dog hated Bonfire Night, but for the fireworks to keep being set off for days ahead and for days afterwards was irresponsible.

'Do you want to drive up to the stables?' Timothy asked, as they reached the pub.

She shook her head. 'I'm being silly. If there was anything wrong, Petra would phone me. And if there was anything **really** wrong, she'd call **you**.'

'That's what I'm here for,' he said. 'Are you sure you don't want to give Petra a call?'

'I'm sure.' She stepped inside. 'Let's talk about something more uplifting.'

'How about...I think Harry will move in with Petra soon,' Timothy said, after he'd bought a couple of drinks and they found a free table.

'You do? She won't move in with him? I'm thinking of Amos and their lack of privacy.'

Timothy took a long swallow and leant back in his seat with a sigh. 'She won't leave the stables. Besides, if it isn't Amos getting in the way of the love-birds at the stables, it will be me in the cottage,' he said.

'What will you do if he does move in with her?'

'The lease on the cottage is due up in a couple of months – I'll renew it, if possible.'

'You're thinking of staying in Picklewick for a while, then?'

'Permanently. I love it here. My job is fab, the village is lovely, and my clients are great. And I've met you...' He waggled his eyebrows at her, in what he must have thought was a suggestive way.

'Stop it,' she laughed, tapping him on the arm. 'That's creepy.'

'You've hurt my feelings. I thought I looked sexy.'

'You do, when you're not using your eyebrows like a demented Sean Connery.'

'Ah, so you **do** think I'm sexy?'

Charity forgot where she was for a moment as she inched closer and wrapped her arms around his neck. 'You're **incredibly** sexy.' Her lips parted and she readied herself for a deep kiss when someone laughed on a nearby table, reminding her where she was. 'Later,' she promised, excitement coursing through her, making her all breathless and trembly.

She had no intention of sleeping with him yet, but the anticipation was excruciating and the touch of his hand in hers almost sent her into orbit.

When the landlord of the Black Horse finally announced time and urged his customers to drink up and be on their way, Charity didn't want the evening to end. She'd had a thoroughly glorious time getting to know Timothy on a deeper level, but there was no way she could invite him back to her house to continue their conversation: not with her mum and dad there. Once again, she thought it might be time she found a place of her own.

'I'll walk you back,' Timothy said, holding her coat out so she could slip her arms into it.

'That'll be nice. I'd invite you back for coffee, but...' She worried at her lip, hoping he hadn't taken her meaning the wrong way. Even if she had the house to herself, her invitation would be for nothing more than coffee and some serious snogging.

'We could go back to mine,' he said, then he grimaced. 'For coffee, I mean. Just coffee.' He shot her an apologetic look, and Charity was amused that he was worried she might think he was suggesting something more nefarious.

She was definitely thrilled at the idea, but not yet.

'Just for coffee,' she agreed, and she felt the tension leave him, only for it to return a half an hour later, after an enthusiastic and passionate embrace on his sofa.

'Goodness,' he murmured, panting slightly when they eventually surfaced.

Charity was trembling with desire and her own breathing was fast and shallow. 'Goodness, indeed,' she agreed, her voice hoarse and ragged.

Their coffees sat on a nearby table, cold and untouched. A fire spat and crackled in the hearth, and the room was warm enough for her to have shed a few items of clothing if she'd had a mind to. Soft music swirled around them, a soothing backdrop for her heightened emotions.

'Shall I take you home now?' he asked gently, his breathing returning to normal.

Charity wished hers would, and her heart rate along with it, because her pulse was thudding in her ears.

'I think you'd better had,' she said, 'before things get out of hand.'

His smile was wry. 'I wouldn't complain if they did.'

Neither would I, Charity thought, before she gave herself a stern talking to. But the thought stayed with her all the way home and for a very long time afterwards.

Harry was at home when Timothy returned, which he was surprised about.

'I thought you were staying over at the stables tonight,' Timothy said. Thank god Charity had decided to go home when she had, otherwise Harry might have walked in on them. Not that they'd been naked or anything, but still...

'I had to come back for the van in the morning, and Petra was back and forth to the stables like a yo-yo all evening, checking on the horses. Some idiots have been letting off fireworks at the other end of Muddypuddle Lane and scaring the animals half to death.'

'I heard. I didn't realise the noise was coming from there – I thought it was coming from the village.'

'Kids, I expect, and when I say kids, I mean youths. Anyway, where have you been? It's gone midnight.'

'The Black Horse, with Charity.'

'Have you been snogging on her doorstep again?'

Timothy narrowed his eyes at his brother. 'We were here, actually.'

'You were? Do I have to give you the birds and the bees talk?' Harry laughed, ducking as Timothy threw a cushion at him.

'I think you gave me that talk a good few years ago. It was excruciatingly embarrassing.'

'Yeah, well, I had the talk off Dad; that was worse.' Harry stopped and stared at Timothy. 'I wish he had been here to give you yours.'

'Me, too.'

'I'm sorry I haven't been home more, Tim.'

'Hey, don't be daft. I didn't take this job so I could live in your pocket.' He twisted his lips into a wry smile.

Harry studied him. 'Are you okay about me and Petra?'

'Hell, yeah! I didn't think there was a woman out there who was prepared to put up with you!' Timothy paused. 'Can I ask you something? Can I take over the lease when it's due up?'

'If you want, or we can put it into joint names.'

'I think you'll move to the stables soon.'

Harry snorted. 'I might as well considering I spend so much time there, but we haven't talked about it. She's got to ask me first, and if you hadn't noticed, Petra is incredibly independent.'

'Talking about asking, would you ever ask her to marry you?'

Harry was silent for a while. 'Definitely, at some point. But not yet.'

'How did you know she was the one?'

'I just did. She fits into my life as though she's meant to be there, and when I tried to imagine life without her, I couldn't.'

It was Timothy's turn to fall silent for several minutes.

Eventually he said, 'I really like Charity. A lot. Did I tell you about when I went on my very first ride at the stables? Faith took me out for a hack and I thought she was Charity. I didn't realise they were twins.'

'And I never thought to mention it. How did that work out?'

'I thought she was awfully stuck-up until I found out I'd been trying to chat up Faith instead of Charity.'

'Ha! Bet that didn't go down well – she's all loved up with a guy who lives in the next village.'

'So I discovered.' Timothy chuckled, his thoughts turning to the stables. 'I wouldn't mind taking up riding again. It's bloody expensive, though.'

'Is that because of Charity? She's almost married to her horse.'

'Not at all.' Timothy drew in a long reflective breath. 'I miss it. Remember when we used to go riding with Mum? Then after they died how I used to beg for rides whenever and wherever I could? I miss the freedom, the feeling of being at one with the horse.'

'There's nothing stopping you from helping out at the stables in exchange for a free ride or two. I hear Faith is leaving Picklewick, so Petra will need someone.'

'I wish I could, but I don't really have the time.'

'You've got time to canoodle with Charity,' Harry pointed out with a laugh.

'That's because I really, really like her.'

There was that look again, as though Harry was examining him. 'I'm pleased for you. She's a lovely woman.'

Timothy blew out a breath. 'It's early days, but I think she likes me too.' And with that, he took himself off to bed, praying he was right.

CHAPTER EIGHT

Charity was in the tack room, performing the weekly chore of cleaning the bridles and saddles. It was a job she didn't particularly enjoy but one which had to be done, and everyone took turns, even Amos and Nathan, and Harry had also been known to lend a hand on occasion.

She wondered if Timothy might be roped into cleaning – according to her sister, he was a decent enough horseman, and she could envisage sitting in the tack room with him occupying her sister's chair, contently sharing the same tub of saddle soap.

It felt strange to be at the stables and knowing Faith was miles away. It was something they usually tried to do together, and they used to love chatting and giggling as they worked. Faith had been gone for eight days, and Charity missed her badly. How was she going to cope when her sister was gone for good?

The day was overcast and dull, with a raw north-westerly wind whipping over the hills, causing lips to chap and eyes to water by the time she finally finished her chores and was able to mount up and go for a ride. Storm pranced and tossed her head, trying to turn her backside to the weather, but once she'd trotted to the end of the lane, the mare settled down and Charity could relax.

It was a bittersweet ride for Charity, as she spotted Midnight grazing in a field next to the lane and guessed he might not be at the stables for much longer. And thinking about his empty stall made her want to cry. She and Faith were coming to the end of an era, and although the future was bright and rosy for Faith, and Charity wanted nothing more than for Faith to be happy, Charity couldn't help feeling sad for herself.

'Snap out of it,' she muttered crossly, then spent the rest of the ride trying to enjoy it and failing miserably. And for the first time ever, she was glad to return to the stables and the warmth of the house.

'Thanks, Amos.' Petra's uncle handed her a mug of piping hot cocoa as soon as she stepped inside, and Charity sipped gratefully, hoping it would ease the chill in her bones and her heart.

Harry was at the sink peeling potatoes, looking incredibly at home, and Charity all of a sudden felt shy and tongue-tied. His features were so similar to Timothy's, it was like gazing at an older version of the man she was falling for, and her tummy flipped over. Would she and Timothy still be together in ten years' time? It would be nice to think so. She could look back on today and remember thinking this very thing...

'Is something wrong?' Harry asked, and she hastened to wipe the glum expression off her face.

'Oh, you know...life...' she replied, the heat of the mug seeping through into her hands.

'Faith?' he guessed.

She nodded.

'Change isn't easy, is it?' he said, and she felt guilty for being so sad about Faith moving away from Picklewick when he and Timothy had suffered a far more devastating blow.

'I need some time to adjust, that's all,' she said. 'We've always done everything together until—' She stopped abruptly, realising how churlish she sounded.

'She fell in love?'

'Are you reading my mind?' she half-joked.

'Not at all; I felt the same way about Timothy to a certain extent. I had to let him go, too.'

'Until he followed you to Picklewick,' Petra said smiling as she strode into the kitchen and headed for the fridge. 'Faith will always be your sister,' Petra said to Charity. 'You might be twins, but you are two separate people, with your own lives to lead. Harry's situation is different; he had to be a parent as well as a sibling. But he's right, you have to let her go up here.' Petra tapped her temple.

Charity knew Petra was right. The days of dressing the same, liking the same things, and finishing each other's sentences weren't exactly gone, because there would always be that unique connection that twins had, but it was time for them to be their own people. Faith was already some way ahead of her on the path.

'I'm going to get my hair cut,' she announced, and Harry blinked at the apparent change of topic. Petra got it though, and she nodded.

Filled with enthusiasm Charity finished her drink and headed back to the village. The hairdresser might be able to fit her in today, if she was lucky.

On the way, she passed Timothy's cottage and her thoughts kept coming back to him. His car was on the drive, and when she imagined him inside the house, her heart predictably skipped a beat. That he was capable of making her heart bounce around and her tummy play host to a hundred butterflies was comforting, because suddenly she knew she wouldn't feel as alone when Faith left as she would have done if Timothy hadn't come into her life.

Maybe, just maybe, she'd find her own happily ever after, too.

'What do you think?' Charity asked, turning her head from side to side.

'It suits you,' Timothy replied, meaning it. She looked more confident, more sophisticated, and the sleek shoulder-length bob highlighted her heart-shaped face. 'You look beautiful.'

'Do you mean it?' Charity frowned.

'I wouldn't say it if I didn't,' he assured her. 'I'll never lie to you.'

'What would you have said if you didn't like it?' She was teasing him, and her eyes twinkled.

'I would have said something like "it's really shiny". Or, "at least I'll not mistake your sister for you again". What does

Faith think about it, now you no longer look identical?'

'I haven't told her I've had it cut, and I've asked Mum and Dad not to mention it when they speak to her. I was going to send her a photo but I want to see her reaction first-hand, not when she's had time to filter it. I'll be able to tell straight away if she hates it or not.'

'She won't hate it,' Timothy said. 'Not when you look so gorgeous.'

'We've always worn our hair the same, though,' she said, looking worried.

'New beginnings call for a new hairstyle,' he said. 'At least, that's what they say, isn't it? I'm sure she'll understand.'

'Talking of new beginnings, I'm also looking for somewhere to rent,' she told him. 'It's time I stood on my own two feet. I can't live with my parents forever. I'm never going to move on if I don't move out. I wonder if Dominic's place will become available? I must remember to ask Faith.'

'Harry is moving into the stables,' he said. Harry had informed him only last night.

'You thought he might,' Charity said, snuggling on the sofa next to him. He draped an arm around her shoulders and pulled her close.

'I'm taking over the lease for the next six months, then I might look for somewhere to buy.' He debated whether to offer for her to live with him, but even if it was only a platonic arrangement in that she would have one of the bedrooms and he would have the other, he didn't think that would end up being the case, or that Charity would view his offer in the spirit it was intended. They'd known each other for all of three weeks (not including their first encounter in the cafe) so it was far too soon to take their relationship to the next level, no matter how swiftly his feelings for her were growing.

'Harry has shifted a lot of his stuff already. I'll give him a hand with the rest tomorrow.'

'I must admit, he was looking very much at home when I saw him up at the stables earlier. He was peeling potatoes.'

'I hope I haven't driven him away,' Timothy said. He'd been fretting about it all last night and most of today, in between patients. 'I feel that no sooner I've moved in, than he's moving out.'

'Does he love Petra?'

Timothy was startled. What a question! 'Most definitely.'

'There's your answer.'

Reflectively, he considered what she'd said. Charity had hit the nail on the head.

Harry had tried to reassure him on several occasions, but it had taken someone else to make him see the truth of it.

'Thank you,' he said, twisting around to face her. 'I've been going around in circles and beating myself up over it, but you're right. Harry's motive is love, not a desire to escape from his annoying little brother.'

'You're not annoying.'

They were nose to nose, his mouth inches from hers. 'I'm not?'

'I don't think so.'

'What am I?'

'Stop fishing for complements,' she murmured, 'and kiss me.'

He didn't need asking twice.

And when their kisses deepened, passion sweeping over them, and she asked, 'Are you expecting Harry back this evening?' he understood what she meant, especially when she grasped his hand and led him upstairs to make him the happiest man in the world.

Charity yawned hugely, and briefly closed her eyes. She was so tired she could sleep for a week. The past few days (or should she say "nights") had been notable for the lack of sleep, amongst other things. It was thinking about the **other things** that made her blush this morning.

'Are we keeping you up?' Brian asked, and she jerked awake.

Blimey, fancy falling asleep at her desk! It was lucky it was a resident who'd noticed, and not William, the care home manager.

'Sorry,' she muttered, but she couldn't prevent a smile from taking over her face as she thought of the main reason she was so exhausted lately. It was all Timothy's fault. If he wasn't so irresistible...

'You look like the cat what's got the cream,' Brian said. 'It's bound to be a fella.'

It certainly was! Charity had never been as happy. She had been on cloud nine since she and Timothy had made love, and she couldn't stop smiling. He had a particular knack of making her feel she was the most special person in the world, and when they slipped between the sheets she felt so very loved and cherished – as well as totally satisfied.

Loved and cherished...hmm. He hadn't said he loved her yet, and he might never utter those three little words, she conceded, but she got the feeling he cared deeply for her.

She more than cared for him. She'd completely fallen for him. It might not be the most intelligent thing she'd ever done and making love with him had only exacerbated her feelings, but she'd been unable to prevent the avalanche of emotions sweeping through her.

Nevertheless, she was hopeful he felt the same way, and every day that went by cemented her certainty. In the short amount of time she'd known him, she felt as close to him as she did to Faith. He completed her, filling a hole in her heart she hadn't been aware was there. She could so easily and thoroughly fall in love with him. In fact, she suspected she was halfway there already.

'He'd better be worth it,' Brian said, and she realised he was standing right next to her and had been watching her for the last couple of minutes.

'He is,' she sighed. 'He most definitely is!'

On impulse, she leant towards the old man and gave him a quick peck on the cheek.

Brian flushed and a smile lit up his face. 'You've made my day,' he told her, and she grinned as he slowly walked away.

Fizzing with happiness, she could fully appreciate what Faith had been experiencing. Charity was finding it hard to concentrate on anything other than Timothy. He seemed to have pushed everything else out of her head. Everything except Storm and the stables, but even when she visited Muddypuddle Lane, half her mind was on what Timothy was doing, and hoping he was thinking about her as much as she was thinking about him.

It was hard fitting it all in, she acknowledged, feeling sympathy for Faith. Her job took a large chunk of her time, and although she loved working at the care home, she would have loved being in bed with Timothy more. The same went for her responsibilities at the stables, especially since she was also doing Faith's share of the work. It wasn't fair for it to fall on Petra's shoulders – Midnight was still being housed at the stables and Charity couldn't expect Petra to do it for nothing. She had a business to run, after all, and lots of mouths to feed. Faith had promised Charity she'd make it up to her, and Charity intended to hold her twin to her promise; she was looking forward to spending more quality time with Timothy as soon as Faith got back.

Which was any minute now, Charity saw, when her phone vibrated and she read Faith's message. Faith was coming home a day early because she and Dominic had finalised everything, and Faith was anxious to sort things out in Picklewick. She was popping into the village to pick up a few things, then Dominic would drop her at their parents' house. Charity smiled drily, betting the sole purpose was to get her washing done.

Charity couldn't wait to see her sister, and she squealed with excitement. They had so much to tell one another, so much to share, and finally Charity didn't feel as though she was being left behind. She felt as though she was starting a whole new chapter.

Life was looking pretty good for both of them, and Charity hugged herself with elation before messaging Faith to tell her she'd missed her and couldn't wait to see her.

If it was Timothy's day to be in the practice he normally walked to work. There didn't seem much point in starting his car's engine for a two-minute journey. And if he was called out to an emergency, he used the company's SUV.

Today had been a typical day of skin rashes, booster shots, a cat off her food, a retriever with an evil-smelling ear, a cockatiel whose beak needed trimming, and a German Shepherd with arthritis. All in all it had been a good day: no upsetting diagnoses, no end of life discussions. He'd operated in the afternoon, and the two spayings and the removal of an abscess from a rather large rabbit had gone without a hitch. He'd finished sooner than he'd scheduled, so he was able to head off home slightly earlier than usual.

He let the staff door click shut behind him and he took a deep breath of fresh air and stretched to ease the kinks out of his back before he began his walk to the cottage. If he called into the corner shop on the way, he might be able to pick up a pumpkin (he'd noticed some the other day when he was in there) and he'd have a go at making pumpkin soup for when Charity got home. His home, not hers. She was spending more and more time in the cottage and Timothy was loving it. It was almost as though they were living together, and he hoped one day she would actually consider moving in with him.

Ever since she'd taken him to bed (he'd teased her that she'd seduced him, and she didn't deny it) she had become the focal point of his life. He thought about her constantly, and whenever he did, his heart filled with joy. It had been totally the right decision to relocate to Picklewick; everything was falling into place and had done from the moment he'd seen the job advertised. Not only did he love his job and the village, he'd also fallen head over heels for the most wonderful woman, and to top it all off, the house in Cheltenham was on the market and the estate agent was hopeful of an offer in the not too distant future. As soon as the house was sold, he could think about using his share to put a deposit on a place in Picklewick, and by then he and Charity would have known each other long enough that his suggestion they live together wouldn't seem so silly.

He was acutely conscious their relationship was incredibly new, but he was also confident it would last. They were made for each other. Timothy couldn't imagine being with anyone else, and if what he felt was love, then so be it. Coming to Picklewick and meeting Charity was fate.

Coming to a halt outside the corner shop, he checked his pocket for his wallet. Did he need to get any money out?

Undecided, he glanced across the road to the hole-in-the-wall to see if there was a queue, and blinked when he spotted Charity.

He thought she was supposed to be at work; the care home was only on the other side of the village however, so she might have nipped out for something. She wasn't wearing the black tailored trousers that were part of her uniform, though; she was wearing jeans and a colourful top, and he wondered if she'd finished early for some reason. He put his hand up to wave, but her back was to him, her bobbed hair swinging around her face as she concentrated on the instructions on the screen, so he let it drop to his side.

Timothy was about to cross the road for a sneaky kiss, but a lorry trundled past and by the time the road was clear, she'd finished her business at the cashpoint and had walked towards a car parked at the kerb. She opened the door and got in.

Then she leant towards the driver and gave the man behind the wheel a long kiss on the lips, her arms entwined around his neck. Even from this distance, she looked as though she was enjoying herself.

Timothy's jaw dropped.

He wasn't sure whether his eyes were playing tricks on him, or not. Could it be Faith? He shook his head, trying frantically to process what he was seeing. It couldn't be Faith. Faith had long hair. The woman in the car had the same sleek bob as Charity, so it had to be her.

He watched as Charity eased back into the passenger seat, and the man tucked a strand of hair behind her ear. It was the same gesture he himself had performed numerous times.

His heart splintering into a thousand pieces, he reached for his phone, hardly taking his eyes off the scene in front of him. He simply couldn't believe she was being so open about it. She was seeing someone else, and she didn't care who knew it.

Dear god...

He swallowed, gathered his courage, and with a shaking hand he sent a message to the woman he finally admitted to himself that he had fallen in love with.

I never want to see you again, it said. **I saw you kissing that man.** Then he turned his phone off.

When he saw Charity bend her head to her phone and begin to read, he turned around, tears building behind his eyes, and walked away, agony in his heart, disbelief in his mind and emptiness in his soul.

Charity Jones had broken his heart and he didn't know how he'd be able to live with the pain.

'What on earth?' Charity read the message for a second time, then a third, her mind lagging behind what her eyes were telling her.

Why would Timothy send her such a thing? What was he talking about? **What man?** He couldn't have meant Brian, could he?

She checked the message again, making sure the number definitely was Timothy's, her heart sinking when she realised it most definitely was. There was no mistake – the message was from him.

What had he thought he'd seen? And **who** had he thought he'd seen her kiss?

Confused and more than a little upset, she tried calling him, but he must have switched his phone off. A horrible thought occurred to her – had he blocked her number?

What had she done? Or, more to the point, what did he **think** she'd done?

Whatever it was, his reaction had been over-the-top. Extreme, even. He wasn't giving her a chance to explain, although she was bewildered as to what explanation she could possibly give him considering she didn't have a clue what he was on about or what she'd done wrong.

Tears gathering in the corners of her eyes, she tried his number again, with the same result, and she understood he had no intention of speaking to her.

Her heart aching and her tummy in knots, she shakily tried calling him from Honeymead's phone, in the hope he wouldn't recognise the number and would answer her.

On hearing the same recorded message, she admitted defeat and left a garbled one of her own. Then she put her head in her hands, gulping back tears as she wondered what on earth was going on. Desperately wanting to speak to him but having to remain at work until the end of her shift, she tried to compose herself. She had a job to do, and it wasn't fair on either visitors or residents if she wasn't totally professional. However, she couldn't prevent a tear sliding down her cheek, no matter how hard she tried, and it was just bad timing that William happened to be heading off home for the day when he spotted her.

'What's wrong?' he asked. And that was all it took for her to begin to cry in earnest.

Little fazed her manager, and unfortunately tears were an all too frequent occurrence in a place such as a care home (although Charity didn't often cry in work, except when a resident passed on), so he gently guided her away from the reception area, whilst asking Rose to cover for her.

'Can I do anything?' he asked when she was safely tucked into his office and away from curious gazes. 'Do you need me to phone anyone?'

The one person she wanted to speak to was Timothy, but he was blanking her.

'Do you mind if I call Faith?' she asked, realising the only other person she wanted was her sister. Faith would know what to do and what to say. 'I'll try not to be long.'

'Of course I don't mind. Take all the time you need. In fact, why don't you knock off now? There's not long to go until your shift ends.'

'Thank you,' she whispered, grateful for his kindness. She'd give Faith a call, then try to do something about her stinging eyes and red nose before she went home. She didn't need her parents asking questions when she didn't have any answers to give them.

'Stay there, I'll come and get you,' Faith said immediately, as Charity sobbed down the phone. Her sister didn't even ask what was wrong. That was what having a sister like Faith was all about – if Charity had told her she'd killed someone, Faith wouldn't ask questions; she'd just turn up with a shovel and her unshakeable belief that whoever it was that Charity had done away with, must have had it coming to them.

Charity had attempted to make herself presentable, although holding a wad of wet tissues to her reddened eyes had done little to make them less red, and was sitting sadly in William's office watching through the window for her sister to arrive when Faith hurried through the main gates.

What Charity saw when she clapped eyes on her sister almost made her smile, and it would have done if she hadn't been so upset.

Faith had been to the hairdresser and she'd also had her hair cut – **into a sleek, shoulder-length bob!**

CHAPTER NINE

'You should talk to him,' Faith said to Charity, for about the tenth time that week. It had been five days since Timothy had accused her of kissing another man. Five days since he'd jumped to the wrong conclusion and hadn't given her a chance to defend herself.

'No way. If he was the last man on earth I'd walk past him and keep going.' Charity's breath clouded around her head as she stomped down the lane towards the field containing Storm and Midnight, plus an older mare. The sisters were bringing them in for the night. It was only during the warmer spring and summer months, did the animals stay out overnight.

'But look at you – you're as miserable as a wet weekend in January.' Faith was puffing and panting behind her as she tried to keep up.

'I like January. Snowdrops flower in January and the days start getting longer.'

'You know what I mean.'

Charity knew perfectly well what Faith meant, but she didn't care.

'How dare he not even give me the opportunity to explain. He should have asked me first, not jumped to conclusions.'

She'd said the same thing countless times.

'I agree, but in a way I can see where he was coming from. I did give Dominic a proper sucky-face snog.'

'Ew.' Charity paused at the gate, slid the bolt back, then held it open for Faith.

'And he wasn't to know I'd had my hair cut in the same style as you.'

'Copycat,' Charity said. 'We've been over this. Let's just lay it to bed and move on, okay?'

'But you're miserable.'

'Yes, I know. I'll get over it.'

'When? How? You're skulking around the village, worried in case you'll bump into him. You can't go on like this. Besides, when he sees me, he'll know he's made an idiot of himself.'

'Duh, he'll think you are me.'

'I'll soon set him straight.'

'Don't bother. If that's the kind of person he is, I've had a lucky escape. I don't want a man who gets jealous and is in my face all the time.'

'He had a good reason. I would have reacted in the same way if I'd caught Dominic in a passionate clinch with another woman. If you won't speak to Timothy, then let me.'

'Don't you dare! I forbid you to speak to him – I can fight my own battles, thank you, and if anyone is going to confront him, it will be me.'

Charity clicked her tongue at Storm and called the horse to her. She was grateful for Faith's concern and support, but she had to stand on her own two feet. They might be twins, but they were separate people, and soon her sister would be gone and Charity would have to learn to deal with things on her own.

'I should have told you I'd had my hair cut,' Faith said yet again. She'd been lamenting the fact she hadn't ever since Charity had told her what happened.

'Yes, well. I didn't tell you, either.' Charity said. She'd felt incredibly strange after she'd had it cut to think that she and Faith no longer looked quite as alike. How wrong could she have been? If she'd only had known it, Faith had given herself the new hair, new beginnings talk too, which had resulted in her paying a hairdresser a visit and emerging with the exact same style as Charity.

When their mother had seen Faith's new hairstyle, all she'd done was roll her eyes and repeat the story of Faith falling out of the tree at the bottom of their garden, and Charity, who had been in the living room reading a book at the time, crying out in sudden pain and clutching her leg. Valerie finished her tale by saying, 'Nothing about you two surprises me.'

A loud bang made Storm startle and shy away, her tail held high as she whirled on her haunches and trotted across the field, Midnight following close behind her. Mabel, an older horse and one which was only ridden occasionally, stared after the younger animals with what could only be described as an amused expression. She calmly flicked an ear and went back to cropping the grass.

'Stormy,' Charity called, as the mare who was doing a circuit of the field with Midnight hot on her heels, came closer to the gate. 'Look what I've got.' She held out half an apple in the hope it would entice the horse to have a lead rope attached to her halter. 'Damned fireworks – someone has been letting them off for weeks. It's not even dark properly yet, so I don't see the point.'

'There are some really stupid people about,' Faith agreed, but before Charity could say anything further, a tremendous explosion sounded almost directly overhead, and she ducked instinctively.

'Bloody hell,' Charity swore, as Midnight squealed in alarm and tore past her, only missing her by inches and catching Faith on the shoulder.

Faith staggered, was spun around and almost lost her balance. Charity shot a hand out to steady her. 'Are you okay?' she asked, keeping her eye on Storm who was galloping around the field with her ears back and her nostrils flaring.

'I'm fine.' Faith rubbed the top of her arm. 'But we need to catch the horses before they do themselves some mischief. Oh, no! **Midnight!**'

Charity tore her gaze away from the mare, to see Midnight aiming directly for the fence. Terrified he was going to attempt to clear it, Faith screamed, and at the last possible moment, he skidded to a halt and tried to turn, but his speed was too great. Charity watched in dismay as he ploughed into the fence. The top section of wire came away with a twang, bringing a length of wood with it. Then to her horror, it snapped back and it's sharp, splintered end pierced the horse in the chest.

Midnight squealed and reared up, hooves flailing, his yellow teeth bared and the whites of his eyes showing. Faith shrieked and dodged to the side as he spun on his hind legs, leapt forwards and charged past her.

Charity thought fast.

'Grab Storm, if you can,' she shouted to Faith, as she ran towards Mabel who had spooked at the sudden noise but had settled down again.

Charity didn't often ride bareback and without reins, but she could when she had to, and this was one of those times. Almost without breaking stride, she vaulted onto Mabel's back and grasped her mane.

Urging the elderly mare forward with her legs and her voice, Charity persuaded her into a trot, and she aimed the horse at a spot where she anticipated Midnight to be in a few moments if he carried on doing wild laps of the field.

Keeping low on Mabel's back so as not to upset Midnight more than he already was, Charity urged the mare into a canter and for several strides the two animals ran side by side, with Charity edging Mabel ever closer to the gelding, trying to use the fence on the one side and the mare's body on his other to slow him down.

It seemed to take forever, but it couldn't have been very long because Petra had only just reached the field when Midnight slowed to a trembling uneven walk, and Charity was able to stretch across and attach the lead rope to his halter.

Feeling sick and shaky herself, she guided Mabel to the gate, where she gladly handed Midnight over to Petra.

'There, there,' Petra murmured, soothing the gelding, running her hands over his body and legs to check for damage. Midnight, still trembling, tolerated her ministrations. He was blowing hard, the whites of his eyes still showing, and he twitched and shook, but at least he didn't try to bolt.

'Call the vet,' Petra said, her voice low. 'Tell them we've a horse with a puncture wound to his chest. It's not very big, but I can't tell how deep it is.'

Charity got her phone out of her pocket, surprised to find she hadn't lost it in the mayhem.

'Are either of you hurt?' Petra asked, continuing to stroke the gelding.

Charity raised her eyebrows at Faith and her sister shook her head. 'No,' Charity replied.

'What about the other horses?' Petra asked.

'They're fine.' Charity swallowed hard, her limbs still shaking.

'Bloody fireworks,' Petra muttered. 'Come on, boy, let's get you in your stall and see what's what.' Never once taking her eyes off the horse, she said to the twins, 'Are you okay to bring the others in? Harry and Amos are rounding up the ponies in the top field. I can send Harry down when they've finished, if you want.'

Faith didn't say anything, and Charity's gaze met Faith's wide eyed and shocked face. She was clutching Storm's lead rope with white-knuckled hands, her mouth opening and closing but nothing was coming out, so Charity answered for them both.

'We can manage.'

'Good work, ladies.' Petra's smile was grim. 'If you hadn't had acted so quickly, we could have had a disaster on our hands. Right, I'm taking Midnight up to the stables. Don't forget to ring the vet.'

Faith didn't look capable of speaking to anyone, so it was down to Charity. She didn't bother with calling the practice; instead, she phoned Timothy. No matter how she felt about him personally, he was a darned good vet. There was no one she trusted more with a horse.

It was just a pity she didn't trust him with her heart.

Timothy's heart nearly leapt out of his chest when he reached for his mobile and saw who was calling him.

Charity!

'Um... hi?' he answered, not daring to hope, but hope flaring deep inside him anyway.

'It's me, Charity. Can you come to the stables? Midnight is hurt.'

Without thinking, his professionalism took over. This wasn't a social call. 'Of course. What's the problem?' He was still in the surgery, and he was shucking off his lab coat as he spoke.

'He's got a puncture wound in his chest from a length of wood.'

'On my way,' he said, hanging up and shouting to Celia to tell her where he was going. Used to having the vets dash off at a moment's notice, she nodded and made a note of his whereabouts.

His thoughts were in turmoil at the prospect of seeing Charity again. He'd not spoken to her or even caught a glimpse of her since he'd accused her of being unfaithful. Harry had tried to reason with him, saying there could be a perfectly acceptable explanation, but as far as Timothy was concerned there could be absolutely no excuse for her to play tonsil hockey with another man when she was supposed to be his girlfriend. Hell, he'd even been considering asking her to live with him when the time was right.

It looked like the time was most definitely **not** right, and never would be. And neither did he accept Harry's argument that a kiss didn't mean she had been unfaithful. As far as Timothy was concerned it meant precisely that, and he'd refused to discuss the situation any more, even going as far as sticking his fingers in his ears and singing la-la-la loudly when Harry had tried to talk to him about it again.

His brother had given him a stern look, then had thrown his hands in the air and stalked off. Timothy had taken his fingers out of his ears and had caught the tail end of what Harry was saying – something about Timothy finding out for himself. 'I give up,' had been Harry's parting shot.

Since then, he'd heard little from Harry, and if he was honest Timothy was glad to put a little distance between him and his brother's well-meaning interference.

With his heart hammering, he pulled into the yard and switched off the engine. Now was not the time to be thinking of Charity: he had an injured horse who deserved his full attention.

Climbing out of his vehicle, he saw Harry waiting for him. 'How bad is it?' he asked.

'It's difficult to tell. I suspect not too bad, but the horse has had a fright and he's in a bit of a state.'

Petra was holding Midnight's head when he entered the animal's stall, stroking the soft nose and blowing gently into the horse's dilated nostrils. The horse was trembling, his skin twitching as though a swarm of insects were irritating his skin, and he rolled his eyes and tossed his head when he saw Timothy.

'It's okay, boy, it's okay,' he crooned, slowly sidling into the stall and being sure not to make any sudden movements. Charity was standing behind Petra and he gave her a brief nod, his swift glance taking in the worry on her face and her tear-filled eyes.

He frowned: something wasn't right.

Suddenly Midnight thrashed and pawed the ground, churning up the deep hay, and Timothy snapped his attention back to the horse, which was where it should have been in the first place.

'Everyone out,' he instructed. 'Let's give him some space. Petra, can you stay and hold his head while I examine him?'

He took a slow step towards the animal, and Midnight flicked his tail and his ears went back. 'There's a good boy,' he said, trying to ignore Charity as she sidled past him.

It was impossible.

His eyes jerked towards her, and he let out a gasp.

The woman who he'd assumed was Charity, was **Faith**.

Midnight crabbed sideways, banging against the side of his stall, and once again Timothy dragged his mind back to his patient.

'What happened?' he asked, scrutinizing the animal.

'Some idiot let off a sodding firework in the lane,' Petra said, anger oozing from her. 'Midnight bolted and tried to plough his way through the fence. A piece of wood splintered and caught him in the chest. I don't think it's serious or deep, but just in case...'

The horse was sweating profusely, his black coat sodden, so it was difficult to tell if he was still bleeding, but Petra had blood on her hands and a smear of copper on her cheek.

It took some time and a lot of comforting for the horse to calm down, but once he did and Timothy examined him, cleaned the wound and gave him a shot of antibiotic, both Timothy and Petra were satisfied the animal didn't need stitches.

'You'll be fine, won't you, lad?' Timothy patted the horse on the neck, glad to see he was nosing at his hay net. Midnight began to nibble at it with soft mobile lips, and Timothy left him to it. 'I don't need to tell you to stable him for a day or two, and keep an eye on him.'

'No, but you did anyway,' Petra retorted.

Timothy didn't take offence, knowing Petra well enough to realise relief was making her cranky. 'You'd better tell Faith her horse is okay. She looked terribly upset.'

'She was. You probably aren't interested, but Charity was an absolute star. If it wasn't for her, Midnight might have done himself a great deal more damage.'

'Of course I'm interested.'

'You've got a funny way of showing it.'

He took a breath and blew it out slowly. 'I thought Faith was Charity just now.'

'Huh, can't you tell them apart yet?' Petra gave him a scornful look.

'The last time I saw Faith, she had long hair. I didn't realise she'd had it cut. It's in the same style as Charity, so I think it was an easy mistake to make.' His eyes widened. '**When** did she have it cut?' he asked slowly.

'When she was in Norwich. Neither of them was aware the other had changed their style until Faith came home. I laughed my socks off when I found out they'd gone for the same one, so they look almost identical again. Doing something like that is a twin thing, apparently.' She stopped talking and bit her lip, a smirk growing around the edges of her mouth. 'You didn't know.'

He shook his head. It was now glaringly obvious to him what had happened.

'You're kidding, right?' Petra was incredulous, as well she might be, and she barked out a laugh. 'Oh, my god, that's priceless! No wonder you thought Charity had been kissing another bloke. It was Faith, all along.'

So that's what Harry had been trying to tell him, that Faith had the same haircut; but Timothy had been childishly chanting la-la-la and had refused to listen. What a dipstick he'd been.

'I'd better go and talk to her, hadn't I?' he said, feeling a total fool, but behind the embarrassment a faint flame of hope had fanned into life.

If he explained, maybe she'd forgive him.

Or maybe not. All she'd needed to do was to tell him what had happened, but she hadn't. Had he burned his bridges and driven her away?

Petra snorted. 'You'd better had. If I was her, I probably wouldn't want to speak to you ever again, though. Muppet,' she added, under her breath.

Her assessment was an accurate one. He really had behaved like a muppet. In his defense, it was only because he had such deep feelings for her that he'd reacted the way he had. If Charity had been any other woman, he'd have simply shrugged and walked away, never to think about her again.

But she wasn't any other woman, and he **had** been thinking about her. Constantly. He hadn't been able to get her out of his mind, and he'd never felt so miserable in his life.

He lifted his chin and squared his shoulders. It was time to tell her how he felt.

All he hoped was that she felt the same way, and she could find it in her heart to forgive him.

Charity had been hoping to keep out of Timothy's way until Faith was ready to go home, or until Timothy left the stables.

It wasn't to be.

She'd taken herself off to the kitchen and had one of Amos's famous hot chocolates to soothe her ragged nerves. She was still shaking from the drama of the evening, and was worried sick about Midnight, and those two things would have been enough on their own, but having Timothy so close was too much, and it had brought her to tears.

Amos had put his arm around her and given her a hug, then in his practical way he'd made her a hot drink and let her get on with sorting herself out.

She'd just finished the last sip and was wondering whether it was safe to return to the stable and find out if Midnight was okay, when a figure loomed in the doorway and she knew without turning her head that it was Timothy.

'I was hoping to catch you,' he said.

Charity hadn't hoped for anything of the sort. The last person she wanted to see was him. He'd caused her enough pain and she wanted some distance between them for a while to try to put her feelings for him behind her. It wasn't going to be easy avoiding him, but she'd been doing all right so far.

'What do you want?' she asked woodenly, then she had a terrible thought. 'Is Midnight okay?'

'He's fine. He's scoffing his supper as we speak.'

'Thank goodness.' She slumped back in her chair, suddenly feeling weak and giddy, despite the hot sweet drink.

'I'll...er...go and see if Petra needs any help,' Amos said, sidling past her as though she was a snake ready to strike. He gave Timothy a nervous smile, then legged it.

Charity watched him go with regret. She'd have preferred him to stay to act as a buffer between her and Timothy.

'I've come to apologise.' Timothy walked over to her and knelt by her chair.

She refused to look at him, knowing if she did, she might burst into tears.

'I thought Faith was you,' he continued.

'Clearly.' Tell her something she didn't know.

'I didn't realise she'd had her hair cut the same as you. It was an easy mistake to make.'

'Agreed. But you didn't give me the chance to defend myself, or to explain.'

'I know, and I can't apologise enough.'

'Agreed,' she repeated. No amount of saying sorry would make up for his lack of trust.

'Would it help if I told you I wouldn't have reacted like I did, if I didn't care about you as much as I do?'

No...Maybe...Heck, she didn't know. She glanced at him. He looked awful. There were dark circles around his eyes and she thought he might have lost some weight.

He gazed at her pleadingly. 'It might be too soon to say this, and you might not want to hear it anyway after the way I treated you, and I know we've only known each other for a few weeks, but when I try to imagine you not being in my life, I can't. I'm falling in love with you, Charity.' He stopped and took a breath, his eyes downcast.

Charity hadn't been expecting that. A profuse apology, perhaps. Even a grovelling one. But not a declaration of love.

It was utterly unexpected. And utterly wonderful.

Joy cascaded through her and she couldn't catch her breath with the force of it.

As she watched his expression turn from hopeful to despairing, she forced herself to speak.

'I'm falling for you, too,' she squeaked, her voice several octaves higher than normal. This wasn't how she'd imagined a man telling her he loved her. She'd envisaged dinner and candles, and wine. Definitely wine.

Before she could say anything further she felt herself being enveloped in his arms as he rained kisses over her face.

Laughing, she captured his mouth, her lips seeking his as she melted into him, her heart filled with love and her soul filled with happiness.

He might be right – they hadn't known each other long, but she felt she'd known him forever, like he was a part of her that she hadn't known was missing until he'd come into her life.

'I love you,' he said, breaking away for the briefest of moments. 'Just in case I didn't make myself clear. I don't want any more misunderstandings.'

'Are you sure you're kissing the right sister?' she teased.

'I'm sure. I've never been so sure of anything in my life.'

'Oi, you two!' Petra made them both jump. 'Stop canoodling and put the kettle on. I could do with a cuppa. Bloody fireworks. They should be banned.'

Petra was right, they should be banned. Charity caught Timothy's eye and grinned; who needed actual fireworks when there were enough emotional fireworks between them to last a thousand Bonfire Nights.

And when he kissed her again, all she heard was Petra muttering, 'Bloody fireworks,' as her love for this wonderfully handsome, thoughtful, silly man burst into everlasting flame.

The Stables on Muddypuddle Lane Series

Spring

Summer

Autumn

Winter

Valentine Kisses

The Patter of Tiny Feet

Wedding Bells

Christmas

About Etti

Etti Summers is the author of wonderfully romantic fiction with happy ever afters guaranteed.

She is also a wife, a mum, a pink gin enthusiast, a veggie grower and a keen reader.

www.ingramcontent.com/pod-product-compliance
Lightning Source LLC
Chambersburg PA
CBHW020759190726
48285CB00006B/2105